WHEN YOU WISH UPON A RAT

Maureen McCarthy

Amulet Books
New York

Library of Congress Cataloging-in-Publication Data

McCarthy, Maureen, 1953–
When you wish upon a rat / by Maureen McCarthy.
p. cm.
Summary: Ready to swap her disappointing family and school life for something better, eleven-year-old Ruth Craze is granted three wishes from Rodney the Rat, a slightly sinister stuffed animal that was a gift from her favorite aunt.
ISBN 978-1-4197-0161-0
[1. Wishes—Fiction. 2. Family life—Fiction.] I. Title.
PZ7.M47841245Wh 2012
[Fic]—dc23
2012015626

Text copyright © 2010 Maureen McCarthy
Book design by Robyn Ng

First published in 2010 in Australia by Allen & Unwin under the title *Careful What You Wish For*.

Printed and bound in U.S.A.
10 9 8 7 6 5 4 3 2 1

Amulet Books are available at special discounts when purchased in quantity for premiums and promotions as well as fundraising or educational use. Special editions can also be created to specification. For details, contact specialsales@abramsbooks.com or the address below.

THE ART OF BOOKS SINCE 1949
115 West 18th Street
New York, NY 10011
www.abramsbooks.com

For

my two totally different but wonderful sisters,

Michalea and Patrice.

And in memory of Gabrielle, our beautiful sister

who lived and died with such faith and optimism.

1

They always felt the oncoming trains way before they saw them. The rickety wooden footbridge would shudder a little, and there would be a clanking along the tracks getting louder and louder, building to a roar.

Ruth and Mary Ellen considered it to be good luck when a train passed. They would grin in anticipation, hold hands, and shut their eyes.

"Here it comes, Ruth! Here it comes!"

"And it's coming for us!"

"For you and me, kiddo!"

"Make a wish!"

"You too. Make a wish!"

Ruth had been scared witless the first time. She'd clung to her aunt and screamed as the long train hurtled by, hissing and shaking beneath her like a weird, angry animal. It still sent a shiver of fear down her spine. All those fast-moving tons of steel racing past, only a few meters from her body!

When the train had gone, they would turn to each other.

"What did you wish for, Ruthie?"

"You first."

"An oak tree growing through my living room floor," Mary Ellen might say.

"Hmmm." Ruth grinned and tried to imagine it.

"What about you?"

"Finding a million dollars in a hole in the backyard when I get home."

"Wouldn't that be fantastic! Did you get another in?"

The aim was to make three detailed wishes before the train had gone, but they usually only managed two. Somehow there was never enough time. It was against the rules to work them out in advance.

"That red bathing suit."

"Oh yes, the red bathing suit. Want to know my second?"

"What?"

"To take you to China with me next year."

"Oh!" Just the idea of it made Ruth giddy. "*Please!*"

"We'll see. We'll see."

Not long after that day, Ruth and her aunt were in luck. Two trains were coming from different directions, and they were going to pass each other not far from the bridge. Surely this would be a day for three wishes.

"What did you wish for?" Ruth yelled over the clanking of the first train.

"Let's wait until the next one's gone."

But by the time the next train had thundered by, Mary Ellen was bent over double and her face was white. She was holding her side and gasping a little, as though she couldn't breathe.

"What's the matter?" Ruth said in alarm.

"Just a pain," her aunt whispered, leaning both elbows on the wooden railing.

"Did you eat something weird?"

"No, no . . . I'll be all right in a minute. Let me have a little rest." She squatted down and peered through the railings, and Ruth knelt beside her.

"Did you make a wish?" Mary Ellen asked.

But Ruth only shrugged; something about a big bedroom, painted in yellow with secret stairs leading up onto the roof, but it didn't matter anymore. Mary Ellen's face was so very white and there was a film of perspiration along her top lip, even though it was winter.

"Let's go home."

Mary Ellen lived alone in a big old apartment block near the city. Her flat was three floors up and overlooked a wonderful sprawling park that ran alongside the river. It was always immaculately neat, orderly, and *interesting*. There were things from all over the world dotted around the place. Most were from her many trips to China: painted stones and vases, figurines, paintings, and tapestries, and usually a story behind each one. Ruth loved nothing better than lying on the floor listening to stories of her aunt's travels.

"Couldn't I live here with you?" Ruth asked as they walked up the steps to the front door. "It's so loud and messy all the time at home. I love it here."

"Oh, Ruthie," said Mary Ellen, squeezing her hand. "I have something for you."

"What is it?" Ruth asked. As far as she was concerned, it was enough just being there for the day instead of going to the football match with the rest of her family. She hadn't been expecting a present.

"Come and see." Her aunt ushered her inside.

Mary Ellen disappeared into her bedroom for a while, eventually emerging with a very old and battered package. It was wrapped in faded brown paper and tied with string and was about twice the size of an ordinary shoe box.

"For you." Mary Ellen handed it to Ruth.

"Thanks!" Ruth took the box and looked at her aunt shyly. "It's old."

Her aunt nodded. "I was around your age when I got it," she said. "You going to open it?"

"Yes." Opening parcels was Ruth's favorite part of presents, so she took her time, while her aunt watched. She cut the string and carefully peeled off the heavy, sticky tape. As she unwrapped the box, she noticed a lot of faded Chinese lettering printed on the outside. A rush of excitement hit her.

"What does that mean?" she asked, pointing at the Chinese letters. Her aunt spoke fluent Mandarin and taught it and Asian history to university students.

"It says *Attention: Precious goods.*" Her aunt smiled, pointing to each word. "And this bit here says *Be careful of these precious goods.*"

"*Careful?*" Ruth looked up at her aunt inquiringly. But Mary Ellen only laughed.

Ruth's hands trembled slightly as she tried to get the lid off. It seemed to be stuck, so she slid her thumbnail underneath. Heart in her mouth, she gingerly eased off both sides of the lid and . . . gave a sharp yelp of surprise and stepped back.

Inside the box was a big gray *rat*. It had sharp claws and thin, spiky hair all over its body, and it was . . . *wearing clothes!* Baggy trousers made of faded sailcloth covered its hind legs, and the red striped shirt and serge jacket had the tiniest buttons imaginable.

Ruth was fascinated. The worn leather boots on its back feet and the cuffs on the jacket made her smile. Was it *real?* She shuddered. *Of course it couldn't be.* But the long nose with whiskers, the thin mouth, and sharp white teeth, only just visible, added up to something so lifelike that . . . it almost seemed it could be.

Ruth forgot about her aunt and stared in complete wonder at the strange creature lying in the box. The rat's slightly battered appearance pulled at her heartstrings in the oddest way. Was it a toy? Was it old or young? Sad or happy? The sly expression on the pointed face, the long black tail, sharp claws and patches of bristles, the little hole in the jacket and mud on the boots, even the grime around its neck and under the claws, made it look wise somehow, as if it had seen a lot. It was like a little gnome or a strange elf from a dream, ugly and yet weirdly beautiful too.

Ruth suddenly laughed out loud. It was the queerest, most exceptional thing she had ever seen.

"You like him?" her aunt asked.

Ruth nodded, hot, suddenly, with the truth of what she was about to admit. "I love him."

"Oh, good!"

"Where . . . did you find him?" Ruth asked.

"He was a gift from a lady I used to know," her aunt replied. "When your mum and I were growing up, she lived next door."

"What was her name?"

"Everyone just called her Bee."

"Bee?" said Ruth. "As in *bumblebee*?"

"Yes." Mary Ellen smiled. "But I called her *Mrs. Bee*."

"Was she friends with Mum and Faye too?" Ruth asked, tentatively putting a finger inside one of the rough little paws, half expecting it to close on her.

"Not so much. They were older. But Mrs. Bee and I became very close."

"Is she still alive?"

"No. She died not long after giving him to me."

"Did she tell you anything . . . else?"

"Only that I should be careful of him."

"Careful of him?" Ruth repeated in a whisper. "But . . . he's not real, is he?"

Mary Ellen kissed the top of Ruth's head and went into the kitchen to begin preparing their lunch. "Maybe just a little bit," she said.

Ruth put the rat back in the box as carefully as she could but didn't put the lid on. She figured that after being cooped up in a box for a long time, more than anything he would appreciate some space and air. She put the box on the side table and went to help her aunt with lunch. But for the next couple of hours, as they ate and talked, she couldn't stop thinking about the strange gift.

When Mary Ellen was in her bedroom making a long phone call, Ruth took him out again and held him up to the large window. She loved this view, particularly in winter. The sun was going down over the park; the pink, streaky sky bled out over the surrounding gray clouds. There were joggers and cyclists and groups of fast walkers cutting their way along the paths under the leaf-bare trees. Feeling safe and cocooned in her aunt's warm apartment, Ruth shivered with pleasure when she remembered that she was going to stay the night as a special treat. She would put the rat on her bedside table so that when she woke up he would be the first thing she saw.

"Don't be afraid," she whispered into the small hairy ear. "You've come to the right person."

Mary Ellen came back into the room and laughed when she saw Ruth holding the rat up to the window.

"Will you promise me something, darling?" Mary Ellen said as they stood staring down at the wintry park. The seriousness of her tone alarmed Ruth a little, but she tried not to show it.

"Don't let him rule you."

"Who?"

"The rat."

"The *rat*?" Ruth laughed. She looked down. With his bright eyes he actually did look as though he were listening to the conversation. "Nobody rules me," she said.

"Good," Mary Ellen said matter-of-factly. "Just remember you are the boss and it will be fine."

"Okay." Ruth was puzzled. She nodded, but she didn't understand. In fact, she didn't have the faintest idea what Mary

Ellen was getting at, but somehow it didn't seem the right time to ask a whole lot of questions.

Her aunt squeezed her shoulders suddenly. "You'll have great fun with him."

"Will I?"

"Oh yes."

"Did you?"

"The best!" Mary Ellen laughed.

2

One year later . . .

Ruth Craze woke early to the sound of blaring news radio and the smell of burned toast. As she lay in bed, she heard her father's deep voice asking the reigning king of all things cool—her fifteen-year-old brother, Marcus—if he'd fed the dog yet.

"I'm looking for my spikes!"

"Feed the dog!"

"He's way too fat."

"Feed the dog, Marcus."

"What about Miss Skinny-bum? She's the one who loves him."

"Just do it," Ruth's father boomed again. "We have to be gone by seven!"

"Sweet," Marcus shot back cheerfully.

Ruth pulled the blanket over her head. *Sweet* had to be the most overused word in her brother's vocabulary. And it wasn't true that she liked the dog. Flipper had worn out his welcome eons ago. He was slow and surly and he smelled bad, but someone had to be on his side. The rest of them were just waiting for him to die.

In the background she could hear the Crown Prince of Dirt, Mess, and Getting-His-Own-Way—otherwise known as Paul, her six-year-old brother—whining about how there was no honey left for his toast.

"Marcus took the last bit."

"Have jam!" their mother shouted from another room.

"Don't like jam!"

"Then go hungry!"

Ruth wished time would stand still for just a bit. Lying snug under the covers, watching the light creeping in through the holes in the blinds, she could imagine a completely different kind of family—a cool, polite, interesting family where everybody minded their own business and no one shouted.

The following week she was going to turn twelve. Maybe she'd get something she actually wanted this year, instead of the usual last-minute-panic presents. Last year it had been a slightly damaged supermarket chocolate cake from the boys, a horrible pair of striped socks from her father, and a double pass to a weird movie with subtitles that Ruth knew for certain her mother had won in a raffle. *Thanks, Mum!* The film had turned out to be not so bad, but that wasn't the point. The point was that on her birthday she went to a *free* film that she had never heard of, with her *mother* in some moldy little cinema that didn't even sell popcorn.

The next day her friends had been *embarrassed* for her rather than sympathetic.

"So that was *it*?" Lou could hardly look Ruth in the eye. "That was all you got for your birthday?"

"Well, I got a gift certificate to a clothing store," Ruth had muttered defensively.

"Who from?"

"My aunt."

"How much?"

"A grand."

Lou's eyes became slits. "*A thousand dollars?*"

Ruth could see that they were all impressed, but there was no way they were going to let her know it.

"When're you going to use it?"

"Soon."

"From your *sick* aunt?" Bonnie had asked.

"Yeah."

"Oh." Bonnie grimaced. "That's a bit creepy."

Bonnie's words made them all look a little uneasy until Katy remembered that she was due at her music lesson and the bell for the end of recess rang.

At least Ruth had managed to avoid admitting that her only birthday card, which the whole family had signed, had been made by her little brother and that it was covered on all four sides with colorful drawings of dinosaurs with "Happy Birthday" bubbles coming from their bums.

Ruth closed her eyes. Even a mat to hide the worn carpet would do, or a curtain to cover the holes in the old blinds, or . . . Her small, stuffy room stuck upstairs over the kitchen and the laundry, with its high, narrow window and sloping ceiling, was not a proper bedroom for a (soon-to-be) teenage girl. So when was someone going to do something about it? Dad said that he'd paint it, and Mum said she'd make fresh curtains, but Ruth couldn't be bothered reminding them anymore. Even thinking about it made her remember how she'd loved sleeping in the big, beautiful, sparely furnished guest bedroom in her aunt's apartment. But that was gone forever, along with her aunt.

Everything here was worn and secondhand. She had to share an ancient computer with her older brother, which was such a pain. He was always playing violent games and chatting with his stupid friends. More than anything else, Ruth wanted one of those sleek little silver laptops of her own. With a laptop of her own she'd be able to make interesting friends all over the world and . . . *and things would be totally different.*

There'd been no mention of her birthday over dinner the night before. All the talk had been centered on the boys, as usual. Marcus had won a scholarship to a music school for the following year, and he'd also been invited to try out for the state cycling team. Not to be outdone, Paul had insisted on showing them all how he could now read *hard* books. There was lots of patting him on the back and joking about how he was going to become the next Einstein. Ruth could distinctly remember reading *The Hobbit* in the *third grade*—a much harder book than Dr. Seuss—but she didn't remember anyone suggesting *she* was going to end up inventing anything. The signs did not look at all promising for her birthday.

"Rise and shine!"

The bedroom door flew open and Ruth's mother crashed in like a tank preparing for battle. "We have to be gone by seven, remember!" Mrs. Craze flipped the blind up with one plump brown hand. "So get a wriggle on!"

Ruth could only blink furiously against the light blasting into her eyes and try to pretend she was somewhere else. In her ideal world no one would ever say *get a wriggle on*, much less yell it at someone who could well be still asleep.

Mrs. Craze's short, round body was encased in a figure-hugging purple tracksuit with a bright yellow turtleneck underneath, and she was wearing an old pair of Marcus's gym shoes with gold stripes down the sides. Ruth had to wonder sometimes if her mother ever looked in the mirror, because if she did right at that moment, even she would have to admit that she looked like an oversized Violet Crumble.

"Remember to bundle up," Mrs. Craze ordered on her way out. "It's freezing outside." She stopped at the door. "Oh, by the way, I'm afraid old Flip had a go at your red sweater last night."

"What?"

"You left it on the veranda!"

"I did not."

"Oh, come on, sourpuss." Mrs. Craze sashayed out of the room, her thick gray hair bouncing around her shoulders like tufts of steel wool. "It's not a tragedy, you know!"

The door slammed shut.

"It is to me!" Ruth yelled back.

"We'll get you another one!"

"When?"

But her mother was out of earshot.

Ruth swung her feet over onto the cold floor. Only last week her other halfway decent piece of clothing, a crisp white shirt that had belonged to Mary Ellen, had come out bright pink from the wash. Her mother hadn't bothered to consider that it shouldn't go in with the el cheapo Indian tablecloth she'd gotten at the two-dollar shop. Ruth walked to the chair where she had laid out her clothes—the way she did every night before going to bed—and started putting on her socks. Then she stopped for a moment.

"Ruth Craze," she told herself firmly, "one day your life will improve."

She was pulling on her sweater when she remembered exactly *why* she'd been woken so early, and her whole mood plummeted another ten notches. Marcus was competing in a bike race in a country town three hours away and they all had to go. This was the *family rule*. It would mean standing all day with crowds of noisy, sports-mad people shouting and screaming and jumping up and down as they watched the races.

Ruth ran to the bedroom door, her pajama bottoms flapping around the calves of her long legs, hoping against hope that there might be some way out of it.

"Do I have to go today?" she called down the hallway.

"Of course you have to come, Ruth!" her mother called back.

"I could stay and clean the house."

"Oh, don't be silly!"

"I could do your accounts." Ruth was the only one in her family with a head for figures. "You and Dad are way behind with your taxes."

"Worrywart!"

"I'm not!"

"Marcus might get into the state team," her mother called. "He needs us all to cheer him on!"

"Hey, Ruth, do you know where my long black socks are?" her father cut in. "You know, the ones that—"

"In the washing basket," Ruth shouted back. *Where do you think they'd be . . . on the roof?*

Ruth was also the only one in the family who could ever find anything.

"Not here!" her father called. "Hey, Ruthie, they're not here."

Fully dressed now, in jeans and her least-favorite pale yellow sweater, Ruth turned off the light and went to the window. Outside, the day was breaking nicely.

She sighed and wondered for the millionth time what terrible thing she might have done in a previous life to be left alone with this messy, absentminded family.

Her father was a paint salesman who thought he was an inventor. He spent every spare moment experimenting with new creations that he was sure would catapult the family into instant wealth. Last year it had been pumpkin-flavored ice cream and cardboard chopsticks; this year it was a tea bag that didn't go soggy in water, along with flavored disposable pens for those who wanted to chew while they were writing! Meanwhile, there was no money for anything. None of his schemes had made the Craze family even one dollar—in fact, they *cost* money, and the big shed at the back of the family home was testament to that. It was full of his failed inventions. There were bits and pieces of them all over the house as well. But in spite of all the spectacular failures, he had a business card that said *Mr. Kenneth Craze: Entrepreneur and Inventor.*

"Dad, you're a salesman!" Ruth sometimes felt compelled to remind him. "Why don't you concentrate on that?"

But he would just smile in that vague, dopey way he had when he wanted to get out of an awkward situation. "I know, Ruthie. I know. But one day it's going to change, you'll see."

Her mother was worse, if that was possible. She was a part-time social worker, always puffing around and running late and getting outraged at the government over something. When she wasn't at work or running after Marcus and Paul, she was in the other half of the back shed covered in wet clay, chucking lumps of it onto the wheel and trying to be an artist.

"Mum, when are you going to make something we can sell?" Ruth often asked grimly. Ruth knew that nothing her mother made was in any way *sellable*, but she needed to make the point that there should be some purpose to all those hours her mother spent in the shed.

All her friends had nice houses, and rooms with matching furniture and pretty bedspreads and expensive toys that they left strewn about like they were nothing. Most of them had mobile phones and computers and sometimes even their own televisions as well. Their parents seemed perfectly content to be secretaries and pilots and nurses and teachers and doctors and lawyers. Why was she the only one without a nice, quiet place to read and do her homework? Her parents were always telling her to invite her friends over, but Ruth never did. Everything was worn and grimy, tattered and old. There was no cable TV and no

DVD player, and there was hardly ever anything really nice to eat.

"Can you come and find my socks, Ruth?" her father shouted. "We've only got fifteen minutes."

"Coming!"

On her way down to the kitchen, Ruth stopped in front of the cracked mirror in the hallway. She looked exactly how she felt on the inside: serious and wary. She tried a smile, but it made her look nervous rather than pleased, tense rather than glad.

She shoved her hair back from her face with both hands and leaned in closer, trying to work out what someone who didn't know her would think. *What would a stranger think of Ruth Craze?*

There was nothing exactly *wrong* with her face. No recessed chin, unsightly bumps, splotchy skin, or dark birthmarks, but there wasn't much right about it, either. Her chin was pointy and her mouth small and straight, her forehead high and her neck thin. *A hard mouth,* Ruth thought, *like a mean old woman in a fairy tale.* At least her eyes were an interesting color, greenish gray like the leaves of a eucalyptus tree. They were large and fringed with heavy, dark lashes. Ruth let her hair fall down around her face again and took a step back, deciding that *plain* would be the best description. She was like any other tall, plain girl standing on the road waiting for a bus. The nice eyes were probably meant for somebody else.

The week before, she'd heard her mother talking to her sister Faye. *What can I do with her?* her mother had moaned. *She won't even smile anymore.*

She's going through a gawky stage. Auntie Faye had sighed, as if she knew all about it.

Gawky. Ruth didn't like that word one little bit.

She turned sideways to try to get a look at the nose that her former best friend Lou had told her was "beaky." Did that mean it was too long or that it was the wrong shape or that she really did look like a bird? Her dark hair was long, thick, and straight. Before she fell out with her friends, she had been rather proud of it, and of the fact that she was tall. Now every time they passed her in the corridor or on the playground, they'd hiss something like *beanpole* under their breath, or *skinny arse.*

The boys were more straightforward. *What's the weather like up there?* they'd yell at her on their way out to smash each other at cricket. The latest rumor around the school was that she was bulimic. *Hey, Ruth, why don't you go chuck up?* That would be funny if it weren't so absolutely *not* the case. Ruth ate a lot, and she never chucked up even when she felt sick or had a pain in the stomach. But she never told any of them that. She never said anything.

Ruth pulled up her hair in an elastic band and went back to the main subject that had been preoccupying her on and off for the last ten months. *Why . . . why . . . why . . . ?* Why did Mary

Ellen have to die when there were so many horrible people still left alive in the world? Why did her quiet, funny, young, pretty, soft-speaking, tall and slim and *interesting* aunt, who was ten years younger than Auntie Faye and seven years younger than Ruth's own mother and who—it had to be said—had been Ruth's favorite person in the whole world, die, when all the mean, cruel, boring ones were left alive? It wasn't right. It wasn't fair. It didn't make sense at all. But there was no getting away from it. She was dead.

Ruth walked into the kitchen to find her father sitting at the table eating a bowl of cereal and staring blankly at the blaring television. Some man in a suit was saying that the stock market had crashed, and her dad was shaking his head. Ruth knew for a fact that Mr. Craze didn't have money invested, *so why should he care?*

Her mother was making sandwiches. Marcus was doing stretches as he waited for his toast to cook, and Paul was eating cereal with one hand and trying to make some kind of construction out of the three or four bits of toast on his plate with the other.

"Hi, Ruthie." Paul smiled through a mouthful of Weetabix.

"Hi, Paul."

"How many inches did you grow last night?"

"Shut up, moonface." Ruth slunk past into the laundry.

"Mum, she called me moonface!"

"Ruth." Mrs. Craze sighed. "Don't tease him."

"He started it!"

"Be proud of your height, Ruth." Mrs. Craze pulled a cardboard box out from under the table. "I wish I had some of it."

"Yeah," Ruth muttered under her breath. Everyone wanted to be tall, except when they *were* tall and getting taller and didn't know when they were going to stop getting taller still. What if she grew into one of those freaks who had to buy their clothes in a special tall women's shop? Her little brother's round face was actually quite cute, but she had to pick on him about something when he turned smart on her.

She pulled a pair of long black socks out of the bottom of the washing basket and held them up for her father to see.

"Oh, thanks," he said distractedly. "Where were they?"

"In the basket."

"Sweet," her father said, and then grinned at her as if he'd said something hilarious.

Ruth frowned. Her father's attempts to be funny were always so totally pathetic. She went to the sink and washed herself a bowl and a spoon from last night's pile of dirty dishes. Next he'd be saying *wicked* or *sick* or . . . *radical*. Last week he'd said *Don't get bent, Ruthie* when she'd complained about the bread being stale. It had been so excruciating, she'd had to leave the room.

"Have you seen your father's wallet?" her mother asked. "He left it here last night. You were cleaning up last night."

"No," Ruth said, and then had a bet with herself that there would be no milk left, which would mean her having to go to the shop, which in turn would mean the usual scrounging around for coins in the bottom of bags and in pockets because there wouldn't be any money left after takeout the night before, this not being pay week. Sometimes it was less trouble to not have any breakfast at all.

"Please *think*, Ruth!" her father begged without taking his eyes off the screen.

"I *am* thinking!" Ruth said indignantly, opening the fridge door. Wonder of wonders! At least half a liter left. She pulled the container out and set it on the table, then plonked herself down, filled her bowl with cereal, and began to pour the milk.

"She never does anything *but* think," Marcus sniggered.

"He's got a point there," her father said, still not taking his eyes off the television. "You do think too much, Ruthie!"

"No I don't."

"Well, you're always frowning."

"No I'm not!"

"Thinking too much can give you headaches." Mrs. Craze turned from where she was putting the piles of sandwiches into plastic ice-cream containers. "It's been proved."

"By who?" Ruth asked.

"The statistics are *everywhere*," her mother declared with an airy laugh.

Ruth gave her mother a hard look. *Was she serious?*

"So I get sick and I die," she mumbled. "Sweet."

"Don't be such a glum bum." Her mother sighed again. "I was *joking.*"

"No you weren't."

"Yes I was."

Marcus was lying on the floor in his bright green Lycra racing gear, raising each leg slowly before lowering it again, his face red with exertion. Suddenly, he stopped what he was doing and sat up.

"I'm going to need someone to hold my stuff and refill my water bottle while the race is on," he exclaimed. "I forgot to organize it."

"Oh, darling, I'd love to," Mrs. Craze said, "but I'll be working the hot dog stand."

"Dad?"

"I'm going to be up in the judge's pavilion," Mr. Craze said. "Remember they asked me?"

"What am I going to do? I'll be the only one without support."

"Calm down," Mr. Craze said. "It will work out."

"How?"

"We'll find someone!"

"What about her?" Marcus said, pointing at Ruth.

They all turned around to where Ruth was sitting quietly at the table trying to eat her breakfast and disappear into thin air at the same time. She'd been half expecting something like this to happen.

"Oh yes. That's a good idea," Mrs. Craze said breezily. "Ruth can do it. Wonderful. That solves that."

"No," Ruth snapped, taking a huge mouthful of cereal.

"Why not?"

"Why should I?" Ruth tried to swallow her food. "I'm not interested in cycling."

"Honey, it will give you something to do," Mrs. Craze said encouragingly, above the din of the weather forecast. "You always say you're bored at these events."

"No."

"*Ruth!*" Mr. and Mrs. Craze, Marcus, and Paul howled indignantly.

"It's your brother!" her mother begged.

"So?"

"You can help him out."

"When does he ever help me out?" Ruth grumbled.

"It won't hurt you." Her father stared at her over his glasses. "It's only a few hours. Don't be a drama queen!"

"Do you have any idea how long *a few hours* is when you're doing something you hate doing?" Ruth said sourly.

For some reason both her parents burst out laughing.

"We do actually, Ruthie," her father said.

"What else were you planning to do?" Marcus grinned. "Sneak

off with a book?" He looked around at the others. "Remember the concert last year!"

"I didn't read while *you* were playing!" Ruth retorted.

"Still, it wasn't very nice," Mrs. Craze said gravely. "Not very nice when a whole lot of people who have practiced all year are trying their hardest and giving their all."

Ruth rolled her eyes and took another mouthful of cereal. *Not very nice?* That concert had gone on for *hours*! So what if she'd quietly read a book? What harm did it do?

"It's not fair," Ruth exploded. "He would never do it for me!"

"But you don't ride," Paul chipped in, "so how can he?"

"Be quiet, Paul!"

"No offense, Ruth, but you've got no friends," Marcus said lightly. "So what else *would* you do?"

Ruth gulped and stared at him for a moment before turning away.

There was an odd pause, and they all stopped what they were doing. Her father turned down the television, looked questioningly at Ruth and then at his wife, then to Marcus and back to Ruth.

Ruth could feel a blast of heat rushing up into her cheeks. She was filled with a sudden wild urge to chuck her bowl straight at her brother's head. How nice it would be to see all the slushy cereal sliding down his acne-spotted face.

"Ruth has friends," she heard her father say.

"She doesn't," Marcus said quietly as he examined a hole in his sport sock.

"What about Lou and ... those other nice girls?" Mrs. Craze asked uncertainly.

"They don't like her anymore," Marcus informed them.

Ruth stuffed another spoonful of Weetabix into her mouth to ward off the misery rising in her chest. She stared at the wall in front of her as she chewed. *As though they knew anything about her! As though any of them had any idea what her real life was like!* Even if she sat them down and told them everything that went on at school, they wouldn't get it. She took another spoonful and tried to think about something nice. A trip to Disneyland would be good. Her own bungalow out back with separate kitchen facilities would be even better.

"Well ... Marcus might get on the state team!" her mother blathered on as she handed him a protein drink in a huge plastic mug. "He needs our support."

"Otherwise, I'll start taking drugs." Marcus winked at Ruth, who stared back stone-faced.

Typical. He always tried to undo mean stuff with some stupid joke.

"Glad that's sorted out, then." Mr. Craze pushed his empty bowl away and stood up. "Marcus, you be sure to pay your sister back sometime, you hear?"

"Sweet," Marcus said, and went back to flexing his calf muscles.

Ruth shifted position and her foot hit something under the table. She bent down, picked up the wallet, and handed it silently to her father.

"Oh, you're a gem, Ruthie!" His eyes lit up. "Thanks, love."

"Well done, Ruthie!" Her mother beamed at her. "You really are a whiz, darling."

Ruth shrugged. All the *gems* and *whiz darlings* in the world did not make up for the fact that she did not want to be in this shambles of a kitchen—why was there a red plastic football on top of the fridge, for example, and why were there strips of greasy paint hanging from the ceiling?—at such an unearthly hour with any of these people whom she was apparently required to help out and be kind to, for no other reason than that they were her family. Ruth frowned. *Family.* As far as she was concerned, family was completely and utterly overrated. She lowered her head and tried to think of something more pleasant. How come being an orphan got such a bad rap? In every book, play, and film, it was the orphan you had to feel sorry for. Ruth could think of at least half a dozen things about being an orphan that would be wonderful.

While she was finishing her cereal a small, wayward idea disassociated itself from the pack of old, boring ones in Ruth's head and raced to the front. *Where had it come from?* Nobody, least of all Ruth, asked for it to start pinging like an electronic bleeper. It had arrived for no obvious reason, and it was different from any idea she'd ever had before. More importantly, it was *growing*.

The longer she sat there looking at all the dirty dishes on the table, knowing it was more than likely that she would be the one to clear away and wash up, the stronger it got. *If you really want something, then . . . you've got to make it happen.* She could almost hear Mary Ellen's voice in her head, and that sent a shiver of excitement down her spine.

All of a sudden, her mouth opened and the words tumbled out before she could even think.

"I can't do it," she said quite firmly, getting up and taking a pile of dishes from the table to the sink.

"Can't do what?" Marcus stopped what he was doing on the floor and turned around.

"I can't come today," Ruth said, hardly able to believe herself.

Mr. Craze turned off the television and Mrs. Craze straightened up from packing food into the cardboard box.

Paul stopped whistling and playing with his toast. In fact, amazingly, the kitchen went quiet all over again. Ruth turned her back and filled the sink with water, aware that they were all looking at her.

"What did you say, Ruth?" Mr. Craze asked.

"Sorry, I forgot. I can't come today," Ruth said calmly, only half turning around. Her heart was hammering in her chest. *What would she say now?*

"Why not?" Marcus was outraged.

"I completely forgot that I have plans with Lou's family."

"Plans with *who*?"

"What are you talking about?"

"Don't be ridiculous, Ruth!"

"And I can't get out of it," Ruth blundered on. "Look, I would have told you before. I just forgot. This has taken me by surprise too."

"What *kind* of plans?" Mr. Craze asked, openmouthed.

"Lou's grandfather had a massive heart operation yesterday," Ruth said, squirting some detergent into the sink. "He's in intensive care. Lou wants me to come and stay with her while her parents go and sit with him all day at the hospital."

Ruth could feel her family staring at her back.

"I'm a . . . close family friend." This last part was true in a sense. Even though she and Lou had fallen out, Lou's parents still probably loved her. Ruth knew they thought she was a good, steady influence on their little princess.

"But, Ruth," her mother said, bewildered by this sudden turn of events, "why wouldn't Lou want to be with them at the hospital?"

"Her parents think hanging around the hospital is . . . damaging," Ruth said. She had no idea where any of this was leading. But the memory of hanging around hospital waiting rooms when Mary Ellen was sick had floated up from nowhere. It had been mind-numbingly boring as well as heartbreaking.

"Damaging?" Mrs. Craze spluttered.

"To Lou's young psyche," Ruth said, nodding seriously.

"Her *what*?" Mrs. Craze shook her head. "Where in heaven do you get such terms? Why didn't you tell us?"

"I just told you, I forgot," Ruth said, turning around.

They were all staring at her blank-faced.

She decided to go for broke. "Ring them if you want to check."

Mr. and Mrs. Craze looked at each other, then at Marcus and Paul, and then back at Ruth.

"But I'm going to feel pretty mean if I have to let them down at this late stage." Ruth turned back to wash the first few plates, trying to look unconcerned. She usually went to great pains to tell the truth, even when it made everyone else feel uncomfortable. She was stunned with herself, as well as a little scared. *What if they found out that she was lying?*

3

"Well, goodness me." Mr. Craze sighed. "I guess we'll just have to rope in somebody else when we get there."

"I guess you will," Ruth murmured.

Luck was on Ruth's side for once. Her parents and brothers were in such a hurry to get away, they didn't bother calling Lou's parents to check her story.

She stood on the front path to watch them leave, and once the car disappeared around the corner a wave of pure relief broke over her. *Yes.* She was free for a whole day!

There would be no shouting brothers, no raucous sports shows on television, no radio replays of boring football matches! No parental voices bossing everyone around. No loud explosive burps or unexpected farts followed by hoots of ridiculous laughter.

She finished the washing-up, wiped down the benches, and swept the floor. Then she got the washing in from the line because it looked like it might rain. The whole day was in front of her. It was only a matter of deciding what to do with it. First things first; breakfast had been ruined earlier, so . . . she would make herself a little feast.

Ruth piled her six slices of peanut-buttered toast with jam onto a plate, then poured herself some milk with loads of chocolate syrup, and took it all into the front room. This was by far the best room of the house. It was lighter and bigger than the others, and although most of the furniture was worn, there were a few nice things that had belonged to Mary Ellen—the big shiny wooden table with matching chairs, the deep blue leather lounge suite, and the antique sideboard. Ruth loved her aunt's stuff even though it didn't go with the other battered bits and pieces. Actually, she loved it *because* it didn't fit in. Ruth put her plate and glass down carefully on the table and went to turn on the heater.

There was a collection of family photos on the wall above the sideboard. Some were properly framed and others were simply pinned or taped to the peeling wallpaper. Ruth sat, eating her food and looking at them. There was a big schmaltzy one of her parents looking into each other's eyes on their wedding day.

They were both vaguely *normal-looking* in the photo. *How things change*, Ruth thought. Then there was a formal family portrait of the five of them together: Mum and Dad, Marcus, herself, and Paul as a baby. There were a few smaller ones of grandparents and Ruth's mother with her two sisters when they were young. Even at thirteen, Mary Ellen looked by far the most interesting of the sisters.

Most of the photos were recent, though. Marcus holding up the bike trophy he'd won the year before. The next was one of Marcus with Paul on his shoulders at the beach, both of them grinning wildly. Ruth was in the background staring with admiration at them. She could remember that day. It was weird now to consider how she used to think that Marcus was wonderful and Paul utterly cute.

Then there was a collection of Paul shots: looking sweet playing in the sandpit at kindergarten; another taken on the first day of school. All in all, there were at least a dozen family snaps featured on the wall, but only one of Ruth by herself. It was a small black-and-white photo at the edge of the collection.

She got up, took the photograph off the wall, and lay down on the floor in front of the heater, staring hard at herself. She liked this photo. The confident, easy way she was staring into the camera reminded her that things hadn't always been so bad. Someone, she couldn't remember who, had caught her standing against the back fence, squinting into the camera. Rodney was poking out from under her arm as if he knew what was going on and didn't particularly approve. Ruth smiled. Rodney had often looked like that. Annoyed and disapproving.

The words *Ruth and Rod* were written in pencil underneath

the photo, with one of her mother's big exclamation marks at the end. Ruth sighed heavily. Trust her mother to get his name wrong. Rodney was *never* Rod! Never in a million years.

Ruth remembered so clearly the day that she'd brought Rodney home. While Mary Ellen chatted with her mum in the kitchen, Ruth had slipped past them, past her little brother practicing handstands, and up to her room.

The rat was lying right at the bottom of her backpack under her night things. She didn't want to risk Marcus or Paul or even her parents catching sight of him until she had a chance to at least get a feel for him in her room.

Ruth shut her bedroom door behind her and looked around. Where would be the best place? She unpacked her pajamas and toothbrush, her spare undies and her books. She pulled Rodney out of her bag, marveling at him all over again. She loved his sharp little claws, long pointed nose, and spiky fur. On her bed seemed wrong somehow. What about on the little rickety table near her bed? But there was hardly room for her lamp and her book. No room for a large rat. There was the bottom drawer of the dresser. She could pull him out whenever she wanted to play. But that didn't feel right, either. Putting him *away* wouldn't do. He was no ordinary toy.

In the end, she put him on top of the bookshelf, next to a pretty vase that Mary Ellen had given her the year before. He looked comfortable sitting there with his tail hanging over the edge.

She sat on her bed and stared up. He looked so wise and humorous. It was going to be such fun waking up every morning and having him up there peering down at her. She lay back with her hands behind her head and wriggled her toes with pleasure. He looked as if he'd been there forever.

"Ruth!"

"Coming."

Ruth smiled at the rat and gave a wave as she went out the door. She had the odd feeling that he inclined his head as she walked out, but she knew that she was most probably imagining things.

For the rest of the day, Ruth had felt a rush of happiness whenever she thought of the rat waiting for her in her room. And that feeling continued into the next day and then the next. She felt truly and utterly *lucky*.

Even when Mary Ellen had gotten so desperately sick, Ruth knew that it was just a matter of time before she got better. Miracles happened all the time, didn't they? There were a million stories on television about people *beating cancer*. Those pessimistic doctors didn't know what they were talking about. That was why Rodney was there. He was special and he would bring them luck.

For the most part, Rodney stayed in her room. He was the

first thing Ruth saw every morning when she woke up and the last before switching off the light at night. She took to telling him about her day as she got into bed. He didn't talk back to her in any *formal* sense, but it didn't matter because she was almost sure that his expression changed. Sometimes he was amused, at other times angry and disapproving; occasionally she could have sworn he was totally bored by her! They had an understanding that if she went somewhere interesting, she would take him with her in the bottom of her bag.

Meanwhile, Mary Ellen got sicker and sicker and sicker.

Ruth got up from where she'd been lying on the floor and tried to shake off the sadness as she put the photo back on the wall and picked up her cup and plate. Rodney was gone now. The way she'd lost him still rankled. *Better to just accept the facts,* her parents had told her. *Other wonderful things will come into your life, Ruthie, just you wait and see!* But what did they know? Not so long after she'd lost the rat, Mary Ellen had died, and then only a few weeks later she'd lost all her friends in one fell swoop.

Not only that, but her former best friend Lou spread around so many stories about her at school that no one else wanted to be friends with her, either. So what wonderful things had come into her life to replace all that she had lost? *Absolutely zilch!* She was nearly twelve and her life was *emptying out,* not filling up.

Ruth ran up to the bathroom to brush her teeth. She had a

free day in front of her and she didn't want to waste it being miserable. She rinsed out her mouth and straightened up and looked at herself in the mirror; she was still tall and skinny and plain. *Too bad!* She decided then and there that she had to *do* something completely out of the ordinary. Something wild and dramatic that she would remember all her life, the way people did in books. If only she could think *what* exactly.

She toyed with the idea of heading into the city. If she stacked on the makeup and found some different clothes, she might just pass for fifteen and be able to get into an R-rated movie. Afterward, she could sit in a café and wait for someone exciting to come along and talk to her. That had happened to her aunt once when she was in Paris.

Ruth closed the bathroom door behind her, wishing she were in Paris and that her mother had some fashion sense so she could rifle through her clothes.

Just then, the front doorbell rang. Strange! It was still very early. Who would be calling at eight o'clock in the morning?

4

It was Howard Pope standing on her doorstep, a little out of breath, holding something in a black plastic bag. Howard Pope, the oddball who'd arrived at school the year before, whom nobody much liked, was standing there looking dirty and slightly off-the-planet, *as usual*.

"Hi, Howard," she said. *How did he even know where she lived?*

"Craze," he replied with a sharp nod, no smile. "Can I come in?"

Howard tended to call people by their surnames, which Ruth found kind of interesting. When she nodded, he pushed past her into the hallway. Ruth shut the door and they stood in the hallway looking uneasily at each other for a moment.

"What is it?" Ruth asked bluntly, pointing at what he was holding.

"A camera."

"Did you steal it?"

"Yeah." Howard frowned thoughtfully, looking past her

down the hallway toward the kitchen. "But I'm not sure I got . . . everything," he mumbled.

"What do you mean, *everything?*"

"Might need batteries and a cable. I don't know."

"You want to check it out in here?" Ruth turned to open the door into the front room, but he didn't follow.

"You got anything to eat?" he asked in the odd, scratchy voice that always caught Ruth's attention in class.

"Sure." She led him down to the kitchen, wondering if it was the theft of the camera that made him seem so agitated.

"Was it scary?"

"What do you mean?" He gave her a hard look.

"Pinching it? Did you nearly get caught or anything?"

"Nah." He sniffed and stared at the ceiling, then walked over to the window and looked out. "Nothing easier."

Ruth pulled out a chair for him and went to the fridge. He had his back to her now, and she could see that he was trembling. There was not much in the fridge except some cheese and tomatoes.

"Are you cold?"

"Nah," he grunted.

"So how come you're shivering?"

Howard didn't answer but lifted up both legs of his jeans to his knees. Big red stripes like burns crisscrossed the white skin. He stood there and said nothing, letting her look.

"My old man went ballistic."

Ruth was shocked. "When?"

"Last night." He nodded thoughtfully, as if he were finding it hard to believe it himself.

Ruth went to the cupboard above the sink and pulled down the zinc and castor oil cream—her mother's answer to every skin condition known to humankind—and handed it to him.

She indicated the chair again and noticed the way Howard winced when he sat down. He unscrewed the lid of the plastic tub, scooped out some cream with his finger, and began to rub it on his legs.

"Use it all," Ruth told him. "We've got more."

Howard nodded and kept applying the cream.

"Sandwich okay?"

"Yeah," Howard said. He finished with the cream and started fiddling around with the camera on the table in front of him, frowning.

Ruth pulled out the bread and quickly threw together a couple of big cheese-and-tomato sandwiches and put them under the griller, trying to think what to say. Behind her, Howard sighed a couple of times.

"Needs batteries and another cord!" he said, exasperated. "Should have taken the box as well."

At school, Ruth had heard *of* Howard Pope before she'd even spoken two words to him. Within a week of him arriving at the school, Lou's phone had gone missing and was eventually found in the bottom of Howard's bag under his smelly socks, along with Justin Appleton's PSP and Melissa Todd's iPod. The fact that all these items were banned wasn't the point. Howard had stolen them *and then left them at the bottom of his bag!*

Ruth found that rather intriguing, even though she had pretended to be outraged like everyone else. It had made her wonder about the quiet new kid with the thick glasses and solemn face. Why would he steal something and not use it? After that incident, everyone was wary of Howard Pope, but that didn't seem to bother him too much. Or stop him. Two months later, the police were up at the school looking for missing items from the local electrical shop. A toaster, a milkshake machine, and an electric kettle were found in Howard's locker. Crazy! Why would an eleven-year-old want those things?

He was also known to have stolen a tray of doughnuts and fifteen Mars bars from the school cafeteria and then shared them around with anyone game enough to partake.

After that, most kids at the school had a grudging respect for Howard. They wouldn't be seen dead actually *hanging out* with him, but he had a kind of status. He was the official *school thief*. When anything went missing, everyone blamed Howard, whether he was guilty or not. And the most intriguing part of it all, to Ruth, was that he didn't seem to care.

She poured him some milk.

"So your dad beat you?" she asked after a while.

"Yep."

"What with?"

"A leather belt."

"Why?"

"I took a look at his rifle."

"His rifle?"

"He goes pig shooting. I was mucking around with it and . . . he caught me."

"Were you *shooting* it?"

"No way." He sniffed. "He was at his girlfriend's place, and I didn't have anything to do. So I took it out just to see how it worked. It's a good gun," he said proudly. "Worth about three grand."

"Yeah?"

"He only ever hits me when he's drunk or hungover," Howard added as an afterthought.

Ruth nodded. After her friends dropped her, Howard was virtually the only one in the sixth grade who'd have anything to do with her. Not that the two of them hung out together in any normal sense. That would have attracted too much attention. The two biggest losers in sixth grade becoming friends would have meant being hassled mercilessly by just about everyone. But when there was no one else around they would talk sometimes. She could usually find him slinking around somewhere on his own, under the peppercorn trees on the far side of the school or near the library. Their conversations were never normal. No talk of how many brothers and sisters they had or what their parents did, nor, for that matter, any discussion of the school or the other kids. Nothing like that. They discussed general things like if it was right to eat meat, or if footballers deserved all the money they got, or if ants felt fear before you stepped on them.

The thing Ruth liked about Howard was that she could never be sure what he was going to say next. Once they were talking about space and how big it was and he told her that the light we see from the stars is actually from *years* ago.

"You mean to tell me that when we see a star we aren't seeing it as it is now but . . ."

"As it was in the past." Howard had finished her sentence with a sly grin. "And some of that light is from hundreds of years ago."

"Wow!"

Ruth pulled the sandwiches from under the griller and spread butter over them. Then she found a plate and put them in front of Howard.

He picked one up and ate ravenously.

Ruth stood watching and thinking. There was something mysterious about him that she liked, something *unknown*. He never gave much away. Everyone at school couldn't wait to tell everyone else what they'd been doing, or what had happened to them, or what they thought about things, but not Howard. He kept his views close to his chest, which was probably why he had no friends.

"Do you hate him?" she asked.

"Who?"

"Your dad," she said.

Howard shrugged and took a long gulp of milk.

"How did you find my place?" she asked.

"I've seen your address on your schoolbag," he said through a mouthful of food.

"So you're a bit of a spy, huh?"

"Kind of." He looked around furtively as if he might, right at that moment, be looking for fresh clues to a mystery that he wasn't going to tell her about. "That's why I need a camera. So, where is your family?"

Without really intending to, Ruth told him the whole story of how she couldn't stand Marcus's bike races and even how she'd lied to her parents.

Howard made no comment, but she could tell he was listening carefully.

"So what are you going to do today?" he asked.

"Not sure yet," she said. "Got any ideas?"

He took a huge bite of his second sandwich and shrugged as if he weren't very interested at all.

When Howard finished the sandwich, he stood up.

"Mind if I have a look around?" he asked.

"Okay," Ruth said.

After he'd checked out the backyard and the bedrooms, they ended up in the front room, where it was warmer. Ruth sat on the heater and watched him snooping around. He banged a few notes on the piano, switched on the computer, picked up the delicate coffee cups on the sideboard and examined them closely. Then he picked up Marcus's guitar and strummed a few chords, all the time looking thoughtful, like he was on the verge of saying something important. Ruth was still trying to formulate a plan for the day.

Howard put the guitar down abruptly and took his jacket off, then went over to study the photos on the wall. Within a few moments he'd taken down the black-and-white shot of her and Rodney.

"Who is Rod?" he asked, taking it over to the window for more light.

"Rodney," Ruth corrected him.

"Rodney, then," Howard said. "Who is he?"

"The rat," she said.

"I figured that!" Howard grinned, still staring intently at the photo. "So where did you get him?"

"From my aunt."

"The one who died?"

"Yep."

"Is he alive?"

Ruth looked up in surprise. "You mean the rat?"

"Yeah."

No one had ever asked her that before.

"He looks alive," Howard persisted.

Ruth suddenly wanted to hug the skinny boy standing by the window.

"Of course not," she said. "It's just that I sort of . . . ," she began tentatively. "I sort of thought . . ." She stopped again.

"What?"

"Nothing."

"Tell me." Howard flopped down in front of the heater. "Come on, I want to know about him."

So she told Howard about the day she was given the rat and about her sense that the rat knew things and actually understood what she said in some weird way. Then she told him how her good luck had disappeared when she didn't have the rat anymore.

"In what way?" Howard asked, his expression blank.

Ruth couldn't work out if he thought she was crazy or . . . not. "Well . . . my aunt died," she said bluntly, "my friends turned on me, and . . . my family became . . . totally obnoxious."

Howard nodded thoughtfully. She didn't care if he did think she was crazy; she could tell by the way he was listening that he wasn't a blabbing kind of person.

"So what happened to him?" Howard asked when she finally stopped talking.

"I . . . I lost him." It hurt to have to admit it, even now.

"How?"

Ruth shrugged.

5

They had been driving back to the city after a night away for one of Marcus's sporting events. It was late afternoon and everyone was grumpy. Ruth was particularly anxious to get back because her new best friend, the queen of the sixth grade, Lou Parker, was having a sleepover at her house. Only two other girls had been invited. This invitation meant that Ruth was now part of the all-important *inner* circle of sixth grade. Lots of good things like this had begun happening lately, and she'd started feeling lucky. Since Rodney.

"Step on it, Dad!" she'd said in a low voice, staring out the window. "This is snail's pace."

"I'm doing the speed limit, Ruth."

"There are no police around here!"

"That isn't the point."

"Well, what *is* the point?" she'd said under her breath. Ruth was worried about Rodney down at the bottom of her bag. He did not take kindly to being cooped up in small places.

Suddenly, there was the floppy sound of rolling rubber, then a loud clunk, and the car began to drift sideways.

"Blowout." Mr. Craze sighed, pulling the car to the side of the road. He closed his eyes and banged his head on the steering wheel before opening the door.

Without a word, the rest of them followed. Sure enough, the tire was completely wrecked. Strips were sticking off at all angles, and there was the smell of burned rubber. Everyone stared at it in dismay for a few moments.

"What's a blowout, Dad?" Paul asked.

"Well, it's when the tube inside the tire—"

"What does it matter what it is?" Ruth shrieked, kicking the tire angrily with one foot. "It means we can't drive on it!"

"Okay, calm down," her father said. "Come on, Marcus, we'd better change this before it gets dark."

Marcus jumped into position beside the wheel, and all their bags and food containers and bits and pieces were heaved out onto the ground around the car as Mr. Craze uncovered the spare-tire cavity.

"How long will this take?" Ruth was hopping from one foot to the other. "Because I have to get back to—"

"We all know what you have to do, Ruth!" her mother cut in irritably.

"Shouldn't take long," Mr. Craze mumbled, head still in the

trunk. He lifted out the spare and rolled it to the side of the car. "All we need now is the jack."

"Hurry, Dad!" Ruth began pacing up and down. "Please."

She noticed her bag sitting on the side of the road and thought of Rodney lying there under all her things, with no idea of what was going on. Night was coming down. Better give him some air. She unzipped the bag and pulled him to the top and left the zip half undone.

"Oh no." Mr. Craze groaned and straightened up from the trunk, shaking his head.

"What?" Mrs. Craze said in alarm. "What is it?"

"Just remembered that I took the jack out last week and forgot to put it back." Mr. Craze groaned again and let his head roll back in a dramatic fashion. "Can't believe I did that."

"So how are we going to change the wheel?" Ruth snapped.

"We're not, Ruthie," her father replied apologetically. "We're going to have to ring for roadside service."

"What!"

"No . . ." Mrs. Craze groaned too. "Ken . . . tell me this isn't happening!"

Mr. Craze looked at Marcus. "Have you got your phone?"

Grim-faced, Marcus handed his phone over. "Better be quick," he said, "the battery's almost out."

"So typical of this family!" Ruth yelled. "Nothing works."

"We all do!" Mrs. Craze shouted back. "For goodness' sake, Ruth."

"Ruth, would you please ..."

Mr. Craze dialed the number and turned away to speak to the operator. But he had some difficulty describing exactly where they were. They'd taken one of the back roads as a shortcut, so no one was sure. Marcus was sent to find out the name of the bridge they'd just crossed. When he came back with the news that it was called Happy Chance Bridge, they all groaned.

Mr. Craze told the operator and switched the phone off. "They'll be up to an hour," he said. "Just have to be patient."

"Why does this always have to happen to us?" Ruth moaned in frustration.

"Ruth, you are not helping," her mother said sharply.

"*Ruth, you are not helping*," Ruth mimicked.

"Watch yourself, my girl," said her father.

Ruth shrugged as though she couldn't care less and walked off toward the bridge. She was so angry that if another car had come past she would have hailed it and tried to get a ride back to the city. As it was, there was no other traffic at all. Ruth leaned on the white wooden railing of Happy Chance Bridge and fumed to herself. *Why did this have to happen on the one day when she really needed to be home at a certain time?* She looked at her watch and sighed. It was nearly six, the time she was meant to turn up at Lou's house for the sleepover. Everyone in the whole year wanted an invitation to Lou's place and she'd finally cracked it. Now look where she was! On a bridge in the middle of nowhere! She didn't even have Lou's number to ring to explain what had happened. The darkness was creeping in around her.

When she got back to the car, Marcus and her parents were standing to one side staring morosely at the busted tire. Ruth opened the back door, about to join her little brother, who was playing on the backseat. But she stopped in shock when she saw what he was playing with. Paul must have spied Rodney at the top of her bag and taken him out.

"Stop!" Ruth yelled. "Give him to me now, Paul!"

"Oh, let him play with it, Ruthie," Mrs. Craze said. "It keeps him occupied."

"No!"

"He's not hurting it." Her father tried to grab her arm to stop her from getting into the car, but Ruth slipped out of his grasp and managed to snatch the rat away from her little brother.

Paul started howling.

"You are such a pain, Ruth," Marcus said, glaring at her. "Why can't you let him play with it? He wasn't hurting it."

"Rodney's mine!"

"You're too old for that stupid rat anyway," Marcus sneered. "Kids your age don't play with toys like that. You should give it to Paul."

"Why don't you go and ... and try out a new hairstyle," Ruth shouted. "Pretty boy!"

She'd walked in on Marcus in the bathroom that morning. He'd been preening and hadn't known she was there. She'd watched him as he turned his head this way and that, putting on a smile and then a sultry frown.

"Hi, handsome," she'd jeered.

She had stayed long enough to see him turn beet red before she ran out again.

Now Marcus made a swift grab for the rat; suddenly, it was his.

"How much do you love him, Ruthie?" He dangled Rodney by the tail just out of her reach. "Tell us all how much you *really* love him."

"Give him back!" Ruth screamed.

But Marcus was enjoying himself too much. Every time she got near him, he pulled away. Back and forth they went, shouting at each other, circling the car.

"Mum! Dad!" she yelled. "Tell Marcus to give him to me!"

"Marcus!" Mr. Craze bellowed.

Just then a yellow car appeared some distance away. It looked like the roadside-service vehicle, and both of Ruth's parents turned away to watch it approach, their attention diverted.

"Looks like them."

"They were quicker than I thought they'd be."

That was all Marcus needed to up the ante. He began to dance backward toward the bridge.

Ruth blundered along after him, her panic rising to a new level.

"Old ratty wants a swim!" Marcus was on the bridge now, laughing and holding the rat up to his ear, appearing to listen. "Yep, he says he wants a swim! We'd better do what he wants, eh, Ruth?"

"Marcus!"

Both her parents' backs were turned, and she couldn't even hear what her brother was saying now. That's when it happened. Everything inside Ruth stopped as she watched Rodney fly like a bird for just a few seconds, up in a high arc against the darkening sky, and then ever so slowly descend into the river. She watched in suspended horror as the rat was pulled downstream by the current and began to disappear from sight. Only then did she move. Down she ran as fast as she could toward the river, catching one glimpse of her brother's shocked face on her way.

"I'm sorry. I didn't mean . . ." Marcus was running after her. "Hey, look, I didn't mean to let go."

Ruth was only a few meters away from the bank now. She didn't care that she wasn't a very good swimmer. She would jump in and fish him out because . . . *she had to.* He would drown.

He would die. He would be lost forever. There was no alternative. Ruth slipped out of her coat and wrenched off her shoes.

"Don't be stupid!" Marcus was frantic now. "Listen, I'm sorry."

But she didn't stop.

"*Ruth!*"

She had almost reached the water when Marcus caught her around the waist and held on.

Struggling and screaming to be let go, Ruth had a last image of Rodney as a small brown dot heading rapidly downstream.

Once the wheel was fixed, the whole family searched the riverbank for the rat. But it was useless and they all knew it. It was too dark.

"We'll come back, Ruth," her mother said on the way home. "He might be caught nearby in a little eddy or backwater. You never know. We'll come back and have a good look in daylight."

Ruth gave no indication that she'd heard, and she looked out the window into the blackness for the whole trip home. She couldn't believe what had just happened, it was so terrible. What was she going to say to Mary Ellen?

"What's an eddy, Mum?" Paul asked.

But his mother didn't reply.

6

"Did you go back?" Howard asked.

Ruth shook her head.

They were sitting in the front room by the heater.

"My aunt was in the hospital when it happened, and straight after that she got much worse and we couldn't go anywhere."

"I reckon you should go back there today."

"But months have gone by."

"Rodney's a clever rat, right?"

Ruth laughed. *He* was *a clever rat*. It was ridiculous, but she really appreciated Howard's attitude. He wasn't being a smart aleck. He was totally serious, and that meant a lot.

"Yeah."

"A clever rat might go back to where he last saw you," Howard said. "In fact, he might be waiting for you."

"You reckon?" Ruth gulped, took a deep breath, and stood up. She felt alternately sick and exhilarated by what Howard was saying.

"But how would I get there?" she said.

Howard looked around at the old computer in the corner of the room. "Got Internet?"

Ruth nodded. After only a few minutes he'd gotten the information she needed and had written it out for her in his untidy scrawl. A tram into the city and then a train to Geelong. From there a short bus trip. Then she'd have to walk for a few kilometers down the back road to the bridge.

"How long do you think it will take?"

"Depends on the connections, but if you get going now, you'll have time and there'll be some daylight left to get back. You got money to buy the ticket?"

Ruth nodded. She earned a bit of money babysitting sometimes. Suddenly, she felt scared.

"What if I get there and there's nothing?"

Howard shrugged.

"What will I tell my parents?" she added.

But he only shrugged again.

"Why don't you come with me?" Ruth asked at last.

"I can't," he replied, his face closing over. He looked at the clock on the wall.

"Why not?"

Howard hesitated. "Have to go somewhere."

"Where?"

"Somewhere with my dad."

Ruth thought of the welts on his legs and her mouth went dry.

"Where?"

Howard shrugged and then looked away. "I just . . . have to . . . go with him."

"Okay." Ruth took the paper with the information on it from him. "Thanks, Howard."

"You're welcome."

She ran down the hallway to the kitchen and grabbed a packet of dry biscuits and a big lump of cheese, a knife, and a couple of apples. She put these into her school backpack along with two juice boxes, two packets of chips, and a chocolate bar that Marcus had bought. He'd be annoyed that she took it, but that only added pleasure to her crime. Apart from her coat, she didn't need anything else.

When Ruth came downstairs with her coat, Howard was by the front door putting on his jacket.

"Changed my mind. I'm coming too," he said, looking at his feet.

Ruth was pleased.

"What about your dad?"

"What about him?"

"Won't he get mad with you?"

Howard's face suddenly split into one of his rare grins. It was there and gone before Ruth had time to fully register it. She smiled back in surprise, waiting for him to explain himself. But Howard was zipping up his jacket.

"So you're ready, then?"

"Yeah, I'm ready." Howard followed her out the door. "Let's go."

It felt odd at first, being on the train with Howard Pope. He took the window seat as though it were his right, and Ruth sat next to him. But she might as well not have been there, at least for the first part of their trip. He was hunched over, staring intently out the window as though concentrating on something very important. Whenever Ruth said anything, he only grunted in reply. It didn't worry her much, though. She was glad he'd come, and, anyway, she had her own things to think about.

The train was an express. It thundered over the busy city traffic, then past suburban backyards, blasting across road crossings and bridges and past miles of housing estates and small factories.

They'd been on the train for forty-five minutes before Howard spoke.

"Should be there soon," he muttered, looking at his watch.

"No speaking on trains," Ruth joked in a low hiss.

Howard grinned. "No standing up or . . . sitting down, either," he said.

"But especially no breathing."

The train slowed and they both stood up.

Howard put his hand on the sliding door, waiting to pull it open.

Ruth imagined one of his father's big square hands picking up the belt the night before, then lifting it up high and bringing it down on Howard's bare legs. *Smack*. The sound would be sizzling and sharp, like bacon frying in a hot pan. Did he grab Howard tight with his other hand so he couldn't get away? *Crack*. How many times did he do it? Did he stop when his arm got tired? A burst of loathing exploded inside her.

They walked down the ramp toward the line of buses. At school she'd noticed bruises on Howard's legs, but she hadn't asked about them. He was so skinny and pale, she'd thought he might have something wrong with him that he didn't want to talk about. "That one is ours," Howard said, pointing at one of the big ones. "We get off at stop six."

Ruth nodded.

"You don't have to put up with being hit, you know," she blurted out when they reached the bus and joined the throng of passengers waiting to get on. "There are people you can tell. They can get him for hitting you." She wasn't even sure if this was true but ... *surely it was*.

Howard's expression remained completely blank, as though she hadn't said anything, and it made her immediately sorry she'd spoken.

It felt good to be getting onto that bus, as if they were in a movie. No one knew them. They didn't have to explain to anyone what they were doing. They filed in behind a dozen or so others and found themselves a seat about halfway down the bus. Ruth took off her coat and stuffed it in her backpack, then put it on the rack above them.

"Can I have the window seat again?" Howard asked.

"Yeah."

"You can have it on the way home."

"Whatever." Ruth shrugged, watching more people get on.

Howard turned away to stare out the window.

By the time the bus pulled out from the curb it was three-quarters full, mostly with old ladies and a few morose-looking couples dressed in overcoats and gloves, rubbing their hands together and commenting on the cold. There was one girl a little older than Ruth sitting across the aisle with someone who looked like she might be her mother. Ruth had felt her checking Howard and her over when she was settling into her seat. But when the girl's mother also looked over with a curious, friendly glance, Ruth avoided meeting their eyes. Let them wonder why she was traveling alone with the strange skinny kid. She didn't want to talk to anyone.

The driver was the last one to take his seat.

"Good morning, folks," he called cheerfully. "We'll be off in less than a minute."

No one answered him or even smiled. Ruth thought it was a bit rude, but she didn't want to be the only one to reply. She watched him throw himself down into his seat and switch on the radio. Pop music blared out as he turned the key and the engine fired into life.

Outside, clouds hung low overhead and light rain drizzled down the large windows. Ruth looked out at flooded gutters swirling with small currents of brown water and thought of the rain the night before. That steady, soft beat on the tin roof, like someone trying to get in. She had lain there thinking of the world outside and what might be going on out there, half wishing she was there and at the same time glad she wasn't. When the bus pulled out, a rush of excitement filled her. At least she wasn't watching the cycling!

Marcus doesn't do quiet! her mother was always joking. *He likes an audience.* As though it were funny and somehow lovable to be someone who never even *tried* to do anything unless at least fifty people were watching! She thought of Marcus that morning, doing his exercises in the kitchen. *What about her?* he'd said, pointing at Ruth as if she was some functionary who was there only to help him become a star.

And yet it hadn't always been like that. Prickles of guilt poked through her thoughts like little thorns. It hurt having to admit it. She and Marcus used to get on. *You're the one who declared war,* he had said to her in exasperation just the other day, and it was true.

The morning after she'd lost Rodney, Marcus had knocked on her door holding a fifty-dollar note.

"Hey, Ruthie, I'm really sorry," he'd said. "I know you loved that rat. I'll make it up to you if I can."

She could tell immediately that he was genuinely sorry. It was there in his eyes. No one was making him apologize. He felt bad. He held the money out to her.

"Here, have this, and I'll have another fifty on Thursday when I get paid."

She'd stared at him and the money and then shut the door in his face.

"I mean it, Ruthie." He'd thumped the door. "I just lost it. I'm sorry."

"Just piss off!" she'd shouted. How could she forgive him when he'd thrown away the most precious thing she'd ever owned?

Ruth turned to Howard, but he seemed more cut off than ever, hunched over, tracing one raindrop with his finger as it made its way slowly down the pane. She looked past him out the window.

It was good being up so high in the bus. When they stopped at the lights, she could see pedestrians hurrying across the wet, shining road, turning their heads away from the wind. She saw a couple of little kids in cute yellow raincoats and a group of teenagers, soaked through, their hair plastered to their faces, throwing around an orange and laughing.

She liked the steady rushing sound of the engine, the shifting of gears and hissing of brakes and the sudden jolts. If only the trip would go on forever. If only she and Howard could just stay on the bus and travel for days and nights to some unknown place and end up in some big, strange city and live with people who didn't know them; if only she could just start all over again!

That first morning after losing Rodney, she had been the last into the kitchen. Marcus and Paul had already had breakfast and were getting ready for school.

"So when can we go back to look?" she'd asked curtly.

"Back where?" Her mother was sorting through the dishes. "Come and do your lunch quickly. There isn't much time."

"To the bridge?"

Her mother had sighed as if it were the last thing she wanted to think about.

"Look, I don't know," she'd said. "Ask your father."

"Dad?" But he was writing notes to himself at the table. She could see the rows of figures—calculations for some stupid new idea, she guessed—and it filled her with fury. *Couldn't he just give up and go to work like a normal person?* She'd heard him talking on the phone about a new-style yogurt he was developing that was going to be different from anything else available because it made itself in the tub or something. Not even her mother bothered to get excited anymore.

"Ken?" Mrs. Craze waved one hand in front of his face to get his attention. "Concentrate."

"What?" He looked up, blinking.

"Ruth wants to know when we'll go back to the river to look for her rat."

"Oh." Her father sighed and took off his glasses and rubbed his eyes.

"You said we'd go soon."

"Ruth, it doesn't make sense. Unfortunately, that thing is gone."

That thing? How dare *he?* Ruth glowered at him.

"But you promised."

"I know, but—"

At exactly that point, the phone had rung.

It was a short call. Mary Ellen had taken a turn for the worse overnight and they were being told to go to the hospital immediately. After Ruth's mother had relayed the news, she stood looking from her husband to her daughter and then back again expectantly, as though either of them might say something that would make what had just happened make sense. Mr. Craze simply looked back at his wife without speaking, his face devoid of expression.

Mrs. Craze suddenly gasped and put one hand over her mouth and the other arm around her belly. She doubled over as though she'd been hit with a sudden excruciating pain and turned away.

Mr. Craze rose from the table.

"I'll ring Faye now," he said. "You and Ruth go to the hospital. I'll come by with the boys later."

Her mother nodded and left the room.

Ruth pushed her breakfast aside, glad that it was taken for granted that she wouldn't be going to school. So Mary Ellen had taken a turn for the worse. *But what did that mean?* She was going to get better because people did *beat cancer* these days, and Mary Ellen, of all the people in the world, simply *must*.

On the way to the hospital, Ruth worried about how she could possibly tell her aunt that Rodney was gone. Again and again she tried to string together a few sentences to explain how it had happened. *Marcus and I were fighting, and before either of us knew it or could even think . . . It happened so quickly . . .* But how could she tell Mary Ellen that? And yet how could she not! Her aunt loved Rodney the way she did.

Since being in the hospital, Mary Ellen had become even more attached to him, if that were possible. *How is our little guy doing?* she'd whispered during Ruth's last visit to the hospital, the same mischievous giggle in her voice whenever Rodney was mentioned.

Ruth had become so accustomed to the prone, wasted body in the hospital bed that it was easy for her to forget her aunt was so ill. She firmly believed that Mary Ellen would start getting better soon because . . . *she had to.*

Occasionally, Mary Ellen would lie back on her pillows dreamily and her voice would become wistful. *Rats make good use of whatever is around them, Ruthie. They know how to forage and look under the surface for what they want. Life is never quite what it seems . . . for a rat.*

As it turned out, there was no need to worry about telling Mary Ellen that Rodney was lost. By the time they got to the hospital that day, she was slipping in and out of consciousness. *So this was what "taking a turn for the worse" actually meant.* Ruth was totally stunned. It was such a huge change from when she'd seen her aunt only a few days earlier.

She sat back and watched as her mother and Auntie Faye tended their sister. They held her hand and gave her sips of water and turned her over and rearranged her pillows and had hushed conversations with the doctors and nurses. Sometimes Mary Ellen opened her eyes and smiled a little; then she would become fretful and agitated as though she were struggling with something huge sitting on her chest. The nurses would come in then and give her an injection and she'd become easy and calm again.

Ruth's shock gave way to numbness after a while. By mid-afternoon she was not only numb but scared. Her aunt's sallow skin and featherlight frame were things she'd grown used to, but now her skin was as yellow as cheese and weirdly translucent too, like plastic. Every bone in her body looked like a sharp stick trying to push through her skin, and her breathing had become harsh and raspy. Every now and again it stopped altogether and Ruth, her mother, and Auntie Faye would wait expectantly until the air came rushing back in deep, desperate, ragged gasps.

So what was happening? Ruth didn't dare ask. This was her aunt and yet . . . it wasn't. Someone else was lying in her aunt's bed. *But no . . . it was Mary Ellen.*

At one point, Mary Ellen waved her sisters away as though their fussing irritated her and motioned feebly for Ruth to come nearer. Right up close, her aunt's gaunt face became huge, as big as the whole world, the eyes enormous and glittering as though someone had lit bright blue flames behind each one to make them shine. Ruth had the strange feeling that her aunt was actually in some other place, already seeing things that no one else had seen.

"Ruthie," Mary Ellen whispered as she took Ruth's warm brown hand in both of her cold, thin, bloodless ones. "My wonderful girl." And then, with a weak smile and a sigh,

"Sorry I won't be here, darling." That was all she managed to say.

It was then that Ruth finally understood that her aunt was never going to leave the hospital bed and walk outside that room again. That she was never again going to open the door to her flat, smiling, or call out, "Just come up, sweetheart," from the upstairs window. They would never laugh again about Rodney's conservative political views or his light fingers when it came to chocolate biscuits. *None of that ever again.*

Mary Ellen was dying. That's what was happening. *Dying*. Ruth lowered her head onto the scrawny hands that already smelled of some other place, and closed her eyes. When she looked up again, her aunt's beautiful eyes were closed. The rasping, tortured sound of her breathing was suddenly unbearable, and Ruth crept out and sat on the floor near the door outside the ward. She put her head on her knees and let the tears leak out onto her faded jeans.

Very soon after that, her father came in with the two boys, and when they went home, Ruth went with them. In the morning she learned that her aunt Mary Ellen had died in the arms of her two sisters just after midnight and that in the end it had been peaceful.

7

Howard had nodded off, his head resting on his hand, his elbow propped on the window ledge.

Ruth leaned across him and put her finger up to the foggy bus window. She drew a few circles and then connected them with straight lines. Thinking about Mary Ellen had sent a rush of tears to her eyes. They slipped down her cheeks as easily as water from an overflowing downpipe and dripped onto her sweater. It didn't worry her too much, though. Howard was asleep and all the other passengers were facing the front. *Wet cheeks for a wet day*, she thought, brushing the tears away with her hand.

"It's time to get on with things," her mother had told her about a week after the funeral. "We have to move on . . . even though it's so hard."

"Maybe *you* do!" Ruth had replied savagely.

"You're not the only one who misses her, Ruth," her mother had replied.

Ruth knew this was true, but she hated her mother for saying it.

They were traveling through countryside now, soft green paddocks with cows and sheep huddled together under trees. The rain continued, light but relentless. They passed over a bridge and Ruth caught a quick glimpse of a brown river. She wiped her eyes with the backs of her hands, blew her nose, and looked around. The man behind her was asleep and the older couple two seats up were leaning against each other and talking. A couple of women a few seats behind her were chattering quietly about shoes.

Ruth felt Howard shift a bit and realized that he was awake; she turned to him and then laughed because he looked a mess. His hair was flattened on one side and standing up all over on the other, and he was still groggy with sleep.

"What were you dreaming about?" Ruth asked him.

But Howard only shrugged.

They got off the bus outside a service station and looked around. It was a question of finding that back road. It had looked easy on the map, but now that they were at the town, neither of them really had a clue which way to walk to find it. The air was chilly, but at least it wasn't raining.

"You kids waiting for someone?" A heavy woman with short dyed-blond hair, dressed in dirty tight jeans and a man's T-shirt, had walked around the corner from the garage. She stood with folded arms, scrutinizing Ruth and Howard suspiciously.

Howard closed down immediately. Ruth could feel it. He was like a snail retreating into its shell. He mumbled something, shook his head, and began to wander off.

"Howard!" she called after him. How come he was leaving this weird-looking woman to her?

He stopped a few meters away but only half turned around and stood looking at the ground, kicking stones as if nothing had anything to do with him.

"We're not waiting for anyone," Ruth said to the woman. "Except, could you tell us please which way is Henderson's Lane?"

The woman looked from one of them to the other. "What you going out there for?" she asked eventually.

"I'm . . . *we're* going to . . . Happy Chance Bridge."

"Why?"

Ruth had a mad impulse to chuck something at her and make a run for it. What did it have to do with her? On the other hand, why *were* they going out to the bridge? Their mission to find Rodney seemed more ridiculous by the minute.

The woman grimaced and gave a snotty sigh when she saw that Ruth wasn't going to answer her.

Howard bent down, picked up a few stones, and began to throw them at a Coke can lying some distance away in the gutter. With every hit, a little rush of elation went through

Ruth. She liked the fact that he was a good shot and, even more, that he was ignoring this horrible woman. Howard threw one more stone, dropped the rest back on the road, and began walking away again. Ruth shrugged and then followed.

"Head out to that intersection there and turn left," the woman called after them. Ruth turned to see one massive arm pointing right. "That road will get you straight onto Henderson's."

"Thanks," Ruth called back, then grabbed Howard's shoulder and turned him in the right direction. "Come on, this way."

"My bet is you're both up to something," the woman called. "So before you try any funny business . . . just remember I've seen you!"

Neither Ruth nor Howard said anything or even turned around. Ruth walked stiffly behind Howard along the quiet street, not noticing her surroundings, she was fuming so much. But when she caught up to Howard, she saw that he was smiling to himself.

"What's funny?"

Howard gave one of his short laughs. *"Remember I've seen you!"* He mimicked the woman's tone, making Ruth laugh too.

By the time they got to the intersection, they had begun to entertain each other with stories about who the woman *really* was under her grimy T-shirt. A spy? A policewoman in disguise?

They got their biggest laugh imagining her dressed up as a fashion model in high heels.

Howard *was* a weirdo. But she liked him.

After a few blocks, the paving gave out and they were walking along a narrow, winding dirt track. There were trees on both sides, but it wasn't dense bushland, and Ruth could see the small farms and houses that were dotted here and there. After the cramped bus ride and the unpleasant conversation with the woman at the service station, a spurt of energy seemed to hit them both and they quickened their pace. The smells and sounds of the country were making Ruth feel as if a plug had been pulled out from the top of her spine. She smiled to herself. Something was loosening knots in her backbone. *Smile, Ruthie!* they were always telling her. *Get the frown off your face.* She looked across at Howard, about to tell him how she was always being told to lighten up, but he seemed preoccupied with his own thoughts, so she kept quiet. She pushed her shoulders back and kept on walking.

"No one knows where I am," Ruth said suddenly, more to herself than Howard.

"Except me," Howard said.

They smiled at each other.

"Did you see your aunt dead?" he asked abruptly.

"No." Ruth was surprised by the question but didn't mind it. She'd been thinking about Mary Ellen and the way she liked walking at night. Sometimes when Ruth stayed over they went walking at night for ages after dinner. Traversing the inner suburbs, along back roads and through parks. Ruth loved it, especially in winter, when it was dark and no one else was about and her aunt would tell her things.

"But I saw her really sick," she offered.

Howard nodded.

"Have you ever seen a dead person?" Ruth asked curiously.

"Yeah," he said, "I was in a car accident where someone . . . died."

"You were *there*?" Ruth's head filled with a mess of chaotic images, but she couldn't imagine what it would be like.

He nodded.

Then she remembered hearing that Howard's mother had died in an accident. This was before she'd gotten to know him at all. She didn't know if the story was true. A lot of stories about Howard bounced around that school. For someone so quiet with no friends, he'd certainly made a weird impact on a lot of people.

"Did your aunt talk about the rat after she gave him to you?" Howard asked.

"Oh yeah." Ruth laughed.

The world that Ruth and her aunt had developed around Rodney started well before Mary Ellen got really sick. In fact, it started the week after Ruth brought him home. Mary Ellen had dropped in for a cup of tea. When Ruth's mother was out of the room, Mary Ellen had asked Ruth in a playful whisper what she thought the rat might get up to when they were all asleep. It had ballooned out from there. Sometimes the two of them had arguments about what the rat might think about this or that, or whether he was really angry about something or maybe just faking it. It was a game, but a serious one all the same. *Oh, I wonder if Rodney would be interested?* her aunt might say as she flipped through the paper and came across an article on facial hair reduction. *What do you think, Ruthie? Will we cut it out for him?* So much fun they'd had! Ruth and her aunt would try to guess the rat's views on everything from climate change to high heels—*Just had a word with him, darling . . . he takes a dim view of them*—and explode with laughter. Ruth loved the sparkle that would rush into her aunt's eyes when she was pretending to be Rodney. *Well, what else would you expect from a . . . rat!* She'd sigh, and Ruth would start giggling.

Of course, half the fun was that no one else was in on the joke. It was *theirs.* Ruth's mother would shake her head as though she didn't even want to understand because it was all too ridiculous. But occasionally Ruth had the feeling that her mother was jealous. *For goodness' sake, Mary Ellen, stop it!* she'd said once. *You're a grown woman! The girl's imagination is fiery enough without you encouraging her!*

"No girl's imagination is ever *too* fiery," Mary Ellen had

whispered to Ruth when her mother was out of the room. "Never forget that, Ruthie. Keep it stoked now, won't you? Keep it as fiery as hell!"

"You used to hang out with those girls at school," Howard said suddenly.

"Yeah."

"So what happened?"

Ruth shrugged. It was as if she didn't know how to go about friendship anymore. All the secrets and intricacies eluded her. She'd burned her bridges the day they all came over to go shopping with her, to cheer her up. An involuntary shudder went through her as she remembered. After that day, hanging out on her own had become virtually her only option; in fact, it had begun to seem increasingly normal.

Mary Ellen had organized the gift certificate from her hospital bed.

"Sweetheart, I want you to have a heap of nice new clothes," she'd explained as she handed over the envelope. Ruth's heart soared. Everything she had was old and unfashionable.

"Go on, open it," Mary Ellen had prompted.

Ruth gulped when she saw that her aunt had given her a thousand dollars. "But I can't . . ." Ruth stumbled on her words.

"You can and will," Mary Ellen said. "I want you to have some nice things. Your mum knows about it. It's to be spent on clothes and shoes. Maybe a little makeup, if you like. Nothing else, okay?"

"But it's too much," Ruth whispered.

"No, it's not," Mary Ellen said emphatically. "You're growing up. You need a few nice things. Start off with a coat and nice boots. You've got great taste. Take your time and only buy things you love."

"Thank you *so* much!"

"You're welcome, darling." Mary Ellen sighed thoughtfully. "You either love clothes and fashion or you don't. Your mum and Faye were never interested, and that doesn't make them inferior in any way, but if you are interested, as I know you are, it actually *hurts* not to have nice things!"

"Yes," Ruth said quietly, brushing away tears with the back of her hand.

"Your mum is the best, Ruthie, but she doesn't really understand, does she?"

"No." Ruth shook her head.

"And money is tight. They've got three kids and they have to spend on essentials. That's why I'm arranging things for you ... in advance."

A chill went down Ruth's spine.

"Please ... don't ... go anywhere." Ruth was overwhelmed by all she wanted to say. "Don't ... *go away* or anything."

Mary Ellen took her hand and squeezed it. "You'll be fine. I know you will."

None of the conversation had seemed real at the time; even the gift certificate Ruth held in her hand seemed like it was part of a dream. But she didn't know how to begin to tell her aunt any of this.

After the funeral was over, Ruth's mum wouldn't leave her alone about the gift certificate.

"Ruthie, when are you going to buy your things with Auntie Mary Ellen's money?"

"Soon."

"It'll lift your spirits to go shopping."

"I'm okay, Mum, really."

"You need some new things. And you have the money now."

"I know. I'll go."

"Do you want me to come with you?"

"No!"

Her mother had looked hurt but said nothing.

Ruth cringed. The very idea of going into those cool shops with her mother was the stuff of a nightmare. But the truth was, she was terrified herself. She had no idea what she should buy first. To have so much money was scary.

Then one Saturday morning her mother broke the news that she'd organized a shopping expedition behind Ruth's back.

"All the girls will be over soon," Mrs. Craze informed Ruth gaily as she sat at the kitchen table finishing her breakfast.

"Who?" Ruth asked warily. Apart from Lou, who'd been over once—and what a disaster that had been—none of her other friends had ever even *seen* her house, so she had no idea who her mother meant.

"Your friends, darling. Lou and Bonnie and Katy and who is the other one? I've forgotten."

"*What?*" Ruth stared at her mother in horror.

"I met Lou's mother down the street," Mrs. Craze chattered on proudly. "She told me that all your friends were concerned when they heard about Mary Ellen. Why didn't you tell them, I wonder. Anyway, we got talking and decided that you should go shopping with your girlfriends."

"You did *what*?"

"Oh, darling, please." Her mother's cheerful expression took on an anxious edge. "I thought you'd love it. Going shopping with your friends will do you good."

"But *you* don't know my friends!" Ruth spluttered.

"I met Lou that time," her mother said reproachfully, "and I met her mother at the parent-teacher night last week, and we ran into each other again, so ..."

"You shouldn't talk to other parents when you go to those things!"

"Oh, Ruth."

"I don't want to go shopping."

"It's already arranged."

"But it will be so embarrassing! Besides, they've got better things to do."

"But they're your friends. Lou's mother said they're all lovely girls and would be happy to come."

All your friends are concerned for you. Since the funeral, Ruth knew she hadn't been herself. Her friends didn't know what to make of her, and Ruth didn't know what to make of herself. It was as if she'd forgotten how to play the game. She came out with opinions that the others didn't like and laughed in the wrong places. Her friends would raise their eyebrows or give the odd deep sigh to let her know she'd made another mistake. Most of the time she felt they were *putting up* with her. But it went the other way too. Sometimes when she was with them, Ruth only just managed to hold herself there. Part of her wanted to back away and start screaming . . .

"So when are they coming?"

"This afternoon." Her mother sighed. "Try to be nice."

Ruth gulped and felt a fresh spasm of nerves hit her gut.

"Do they want to come?"

"Why wouldn't they?"

Where to begin? Ruth looked pointedly around the messy kitchen, the strips of paint hanging from the ceiling, and her brothers' cereal-encrusted dishes, but her mother's back was turned so she didn't see.

"You just don't get it, Mum, do you?" Ruth whispered.

"What was that, love?"

"Nothing," said Ruth. "So, Lou and who else?"

"All the gang," her mother said brightly. "Bonnie and Katy and . . . Susie!"

The gang? Ruth's jaw began to clench. There were some things adults should never say. She walked out of the room without another word. Just the idea of having all her friends in her house made her feel faint with terror.

"Now, try to be nice, Ruth!" her mother called after her.

"Ruth! Your friends are here!"

Ruth got up from where she'd been lying on her bed and walked down to the kitchen.

Lou, Katy, Susie, and Bonnie were standing in the middle of the room in a tight group, looking around suspiciously at the greasy wallpaper and battered fridge. Mrs. Craze had made an effort, and for that Ruth knew she should be grateful. There was no mess on the table and the washing-up was done. Newspapers had been piled into the far corner along with her father's boxes. It was well short of anything her friends would be used to, but it did look better than usual.

They were all dressed in cute clothes: halter tops, strappy dresses, jeans, and miniskirts. Lou was in pink and had her hair done in tiny braids. Katy was wearing huge shiny earrings. They all smiled when they saw her.

"Hey!" plump little Bonnie squealed. "Love the jeans!"

"Thanks." Ruth flushed. These were her old jeans, the ones she always wore. Bonnie was trying to be kind. *Or not.* Depending on how you wanted to look at it.

"That necklace is cool." Lou reached out to touch the tiny

beads of the lovely black stone necklace that Mary Ellen had left Ruth. Lou's eyes narrowed. "Where did you get it?"

"Picked it up at the market." Ruth tried to sound careless.

"Now, who is going to have Coke?" Mrs. Craze was behind the kitchen bench getting out glasses.

Ruth went to help her mother, pretending this was normal. They never had bottles of soft drinks sitting around in the fridge normally, so her mother must have gone out especially.

"Now, I hope you girls have a nice time at the mall. I have to go to work for a few hours," Mrs. Craze said, looking at the clock as she set a couple of bowls of crackers on the table, "but I'll see you all back here after you've been shopping."

"Bye, Mrs. Craze," they all caroled politely.

Ruth noticed the amused way Lou took in her mother's stout figure in her worn jeans and plain shirt as she walked out.

"Work must be relaxed," she muttered, one eyebrow raised.

"Yeah, it is," Ruth said, flushing even more furiously. "She doesn't have to dress up. So . . . you want a drink first?"

"Sure."

Ruth poured the drinks and they all sat down at the table without speaking. She had a feeling that something wasn't right but couldn't work out what exactly.

Eventually, Lou took a deep breath and fixed Ruth with one of her haughty stares. "Why didn't you tell us?"

"Tell you *what*?"

"That you were so upset about your aunt."

The others murmured in agreement. They'd obviously had *a discussion.*

"I mean, we knew she'd died and everything, but we thought she was just some old relative. We didn't know that you and her were totally . . . *close.*"

"Why didn't you tell us you were so . . . *upset?*" Bonnie sniffed. *When in doubt, always use the same words as Lou.* "Why keep it to yourself?"

"I didn't think you'd be interested," Ruth mumbled. Imagining her mother blabbing on to everyone about how her daughter was missing Mary Ellen so much made Ruth just want to curl up and die.

"Not interested?" Lou laughed. "But we're your friends!"

"I know, but . . . I didn't want to carry on about it."

"You've got to be joking!" Lou had on her deeply offended face. "You *know* I'm going to be a psychologist!"

Ruth tried to look apologetic. In fact, she hadn't known that. Last she knew Lou was going to be a pilot, and before that a vet. From second to fifth grade she had been going to be a top fashion model, but that got sidelined when she didn't grow as tall as everyone else. Needless to say, Bonnie and Katy and Susie were looking on seriously, nodding and frowning, agreeing that Ruth had committed yet another incredible blunder.

"Well, sorry," Ruth said. "I just didn't think."

"Anyway, now we know," Lou said magnanimously. "We're your friends and we're here to help."

"Thanks. It's great of you all to come."

They all smiled at this.

"We want to cheer you up."

"Absolutely," Bonnie mumbled.

"So what now?" Lou said, looking around. "Shall we go check out the shops?"

"That would be awesome," Susie answered for them all.

It *was* exciting at first. The mall was very crowded, full of all kinds of people: gangs of teenage boys, families with little kids, street performers, businesspeople, and ordinary shoppers, girls like themselves on the prowl. Although it was only a quick tram ride from the Craze house, Ruth had hardly ever been there, mainly because she'd never had any money to spend. There was so much to check out, and it was exciting to feel the gift certificate in her pocket. She followed her friends around, staring at everything, not really listening too closely as they laughed and chattered and pointed things out to one another.

Finally, they came to the store that Mary Ellen had picked out. Lou threw an arm around Ruth's neck and pointed at the big bright letters. Ruth stared in at the shining black-and-gray counters and strategically placed spotlights illuminating the racks of clothes. No way in the world would she have ever dared to enter this place on her own, but with her willing bevy of friends, why not?

"Cool, huh?" Lou shouted over the loud, pumping music.

"Yeah." Ruth smiled tentatively. "Cool."

Once inside, Lou, Bonnie, Susie, and Katy split up and prowled about like experts, leaving Ruth floundering, not knowing where to start. Her friends called out loudly to one another, giggling and picking stuff out for praise or ridicule.

"Can I help you girls?" The young sales assistant was watching them warily.

"Not yet, thanks," Lou called back breezily.

"Hey, Ruth, you like this? What size are you? Is this the kind of thing you're after?"

Ruth nodded uneasily. She felt foolish that she had no clear idea what she was looking for or how to find it.

Within minutes, they were all heading toward her with armfuls of clothes and shoes and pointing her toward the dressing room.

"Here you go."

"This goes with that," Katy said, holding out a pair of bright red cutoffs and a tiny striped, frilly top. "And here are the shoes."

Ruth could see immediately that the things they were choosing were all wrong. Nice things, but not her style. They were trying to make her look like them! But she took the first pile of clothes and disappeared behind the curtain. *Relax*, she told herself. Her friends were helping her choose her new ward-robe, that was all. Maybe she did need to loosen up a bit about what she thought was right for her.

Ruth looked at herself in the mirror and tried to get the glum expression off her face.

The first outfit she tried on was a long black T-shirt dress with a red belt. The other girls insisted that it went with shiny, flecked tights that Ruth didn't much like, but she hardly dared to say so because when she came out of the dressing room they were all so admiring. Bonnie brought over a little pink jacket, to go over the top, and Lou started pinning Ruth's hair back with some iridescent clips she'd found. Bonnie ran back for a different pair of shoes.

"You like it?" Katy wanted to know.

"I guess so," Ruth said uncomfortably. She looked fashion-able, she supposed, and that was the point . . .

. . . *wasn't it?* The trouble was that she could hear Mary Ellen's voice in her head. She tried to push it away, but it kept butting in. *You have a natural inclination toward an interesting, arty look, so go with that, Ruthie. You have taste, so use it.*

"It's great," Lou declared. "You're so lucky to be tall. You look at least fifteen!"

And so it went on. By the time Ruth was on to her tenth outfit, the changing cubicle was beginning to feel like a prison, cramped and claustrophobic and hot. She hated seeing all sides of herself under such harsh light. Her thighs were too white and her undies were worn and grubby. Her face stared back at her, so serious and dour. *I'm ugly,* she thought. *I'm too skinny and my ears are too big.* "Thanks, but I've tried on enough," she shouted when Katy pushed yet more clothes through to her.

"Please, I don't want to do this anymore."

The excited chatter subsided into a sudden hushed silence.

"Are you okay in there?" Lou's voice was sharp.

"Yeah." But Ruth didn't feel okay at all. She felt as if she was going to be sick. "But I think I might have drunk too much Coke or something," she mumbled feebly.

"One last top!" Bonnie pleaded. "You gotta try this!"

A weird kind of anger surfaced inside Ruth, and before she could caution herself, the words jumped from her mouth.

"No!" she snapped. "I've had enough."

"Oh, come on, you'll love it."

"No!"

"But why?"

"I've had enough!" Ruth shouted.

Trembling slightly, she climbed back into her own clothes and opened the door. The four of them were standing there waiting. They stared at her in unforgiving silence.

"What is *up*?"

"Nothing." Ruth was wretched with confusion.

Lou rolled her eyes and sighed. "We're only trying to help!"

"I know."

"You have all this money and—"

"I know!" Ruth hardly dared speak. "But I . . ."

"Do you want to shop on your own?"

"No."

"We thought you *wanted* to do this!"

"We thought it would be fun!" Bonnie wailed.

"I know . . ."

"Do you want to do this with your *mother*?" Lou asked.

"No!"

"So what's the problem?" she demanded.

"No problem."

The clothes were wrapped and bagged in heavy silence. Ruth picked up her bags and followed the others out of the shop. None of them looked at her. Something had gone badly awry and it was her fault. No one spoke as they all made their way out through the busy shopping mall. Panic began to gnaw away in her chest. Had she wrecked it all? Undone all the good stuff? She knew the rules. Of course she did. Rule number one was that she must *join in* even when it was something she didn't like. And rule number two was that Lou decided what was cool and what wasn't. *Why couldn't she learn? Why did she always mess things up?*

Lou was walking on ahead in a huff, eyes forward, shoulders back, and head held high. Katy, Susie, and Bonnie tried to keep up with her on either side and Ruth was left trundling along behind, carrying all her bags. She could see that the other girls were waiting for Lou to give them a clue about what would happen next. Were they to stay mad at Ruth or not? But Lou continued the haughty silence and gave nothing away.

At last they were outside in the fresh air again.

"Why do you talk to that weirdo?" Bonnie suddenly asked Ruth.

The question caught Ruth off guard. In spite of the hot day a shiver of cold slid down her spine. She knew whom Bonnie meant, but more importantly she knew why she was being asked the question. Bringing up Howard was Bonnie's way of making things worse. Making sure Ruth stayed on the outs with Lou would give Bonnie the best chance of sliding back into the position of Lou's *best friend.*

"What weirdo?" Ruth asked, to give herself time.

"Howard Pope," Bonnie replied sharply.

They were all waiting for Ruth to speak. She knew in her bones she was meant to say something mean about Howard and deny their tentative friendship. Of course the girls had noticed when she hadn't bothered to find them at lunchtime and instead had hung out with Howard under his tree. The place he always went to at break times. *The weirdo!* This was her chance to get herself off the hook and back into their good books. But something in her couldn't say it.

She was filled with a fleeting but strong memory of standing with Howard under that tree away from all the other kids. She could almost see his coarse hair and the bright sunlight flickering into his clear eyes. Only the week before she'd noticed fresh bruises on his bare legs and had wanted to ask how they got there, but it had seemed too personal.

"What exactly is up with you two?" Bonnie said, feigning concern.

"What do you mean?"

"Well, you *talk* to him."

Ruth was suddenly desperate. She felt like she was drowning, struggling to get to the surface to breathe. What had possessed her mother to organize this terrible afternoon? Why not chuck the bags and make a run for it? Anything to get away!

"We've seen you near the water fountain." Katy giggled.

"And the tree." Bonnie flashed a glance at Lou to see how she was taking this turn in the conversation. "It looked like you were discussing something *really* important," she added in her sweet, innocent voice. "Do you *like* him or something?"

"Why do you even bother to talk to him?" Lou asked.

They'd stopped at the light, waiting to cross the main road. Heavy traffic thundered past only a meter away. Ruth found herself wondering what it would be like to just step out into it and see what happened. She imagined the screeching brakes and burned rubber, the mayhem, the chaos, and the drama of the ambulance ride to the hospital. At least she'd be away from this.

"Since when is it wrong to talk to someone?" she snapped.

They all stiffened. Nobody *but nobody* ever spoke to Lou like that!

"He stole my things, Ruth," Lou said. "Did he ever say *why?*"

Ruth almost wilted under that cool, appraising stare, but then the same picture of Howard standing under the tree slid behind her eyes and it seemed to hold her together.

"No," she said calmly, hoping none of them could see how tense she was.

"Did you ever ask?"

"No."

"Why not?" Bonnie cut in excitedly.

"I just didn't."

"But Lou is your *best* friend!"

"Why don't you shut up, Bonnie," Ruth said furiously.

"*What?*" Bonnie's face turned bright pink.

"You heard me. Just *shut up!*" Ruth repeated loudly. "You're so *boring.*" She turned back to Lou, who was staring at her. "At least Howard isn't boring!"

Bonnie burst into a sudden flood of loud, dramatic tears.

All part of the strategy, Ruth thought, watching her coldly. *She knows exactly what she's doing.*

Katy and Susie moved in protectively on either side of

Bonnie. All three of them stared accusingly at Ruth, as though she'd turned into some kind of monster. But Lou didn't move.

"What's *with* you?" she said.

Ruth said nothing. Bonnie's sniffs and sobs filled the silence.

"So it's okay to hurt people?" Lou said, her eyes boring into Ruth's.

Ruth felt something almost like laughter rising in her chest. *As if you care about hurting people,* she thought.

"We're all here *helping* you." Lou's tone was savage now.

"*You* think she's boring too!" Ruth said recklessly, and then immediately regretted it.

But the damage was done. A gasp of horror went through the whole group. Bonnie looked up from where she was hiding her wet face in her hands and glanced at Lou, who colored up with embarrassment because it was true. Lou's eyes flicked away to the side for a moment.

"Liar."

"No, Lou," Ruth came back hotly before she could think, "you're the liar. You don't even *like* her. You just need a crowd around you and . . . she does what you say."

Lou's mouth fell open. The air prickled with tension.

Katy and Susie exchanged nervous looks.

Lou finally took things in hand. "Come on," she said, turning on her heel. "Let's go."

Ruth watched as the girls marched off after Lou.

She wanted to run after them and apologize, say it was all a misunderstanding, that of course she was grateful for their help with the shopping. But she didn't move. She stood as still as a post, hanging on to her bags.

Lou turned when they reached the corner. "Have an *interesting* life with your freaky boyfriend, loser!"

9

"We're here!" Howard pointed at the sign. "Should I go and look under the bridge?"

"Sure." Ruth was touched that Howard would bother. "I'll walk over to the other side."

The bridge was just up ahead of the sign. Howard quickened his pace and Ruth followed along behind, trying to shake off the memory of the shopping day. The sun had come out and the faint breeze was making the leaves on the trees rustle in a way that was both friendly and encouraging.

Ruth walked out into the middle of the bridge, rested her elbows on the railing, and looked down at the brown water swirling below. Of course there was no sign of Rodney. But she hadn't expected there would be. *So why had she come?* She picked up a few little sticks and tossed them one by one over the edge, watching them spin down to the water.

"Howard," she called, and there was a faint, muffled reply, but she couldn't see him. She scrambled down the embankment and poked about under the bridge itself, searching among the twigs, old beer cans, and faded potato chip bags. The remnants of a fire were scattered about, along with a woman's sneaker and an old newspaper. It was too faded to see the date. Ruth tried to imagine who might have last been down there. She went in deeper, right under the bridge, and shouted.

"Howard," she called. "Hello! It's cold down here." But this time there was only her voice echoing back like an eerie dream. Ruth closed her eyes tightly, reliving the moment when her brother threw Rodney off the bridge. Maybe if she concentrated really hard, Rodney, wherever he was, would receive her message and send one back telling her that he was okay. That was all she needed to know, really.

But nothing happened. Same as when she had gone to visit Mary Ellen's grave with flowers. Nothing had happened. When someone was gone, they were gone, and when they were dead, they were dead. A car passed overhead. Ruth opened her eyes and walked back out into the sunshine.

There was Howard, wandering around on the other side of the river, a long stick in one hand, ferociously beating the nearby bushes as though they had wronged him in some serious way. Ruth was about to yell for him to calm down and stop bashing everything when he stopped under a big gum tree and stood very still with his head thrown back. Something had caught his attention. He stood there for ages, looking up into the branches of the tree as though under a spell.

Amused, Ruth waited for him to come out of his reverie. *What was he thinking about?*

At last he lowered his head and turned around.

"Found anything?" Ruth called.

Her presence seemed to startle him. He must have been so engrossed in his own thoughts that he'd forgotten all about her.

"Not yet." He threw the stick into the water and wandered across the bridge toward her.

"You still think we'll find him?" Ruth asked.

"Yeah, of course," Howard said.

They settled down easily together on the bank near a tree and ate some of the biscuits and cheese that Ruth had brought.

"So what now?" Ruth mused as she picked up a small stick and threw it as far as she could into the river.

But Howard was already rolling up his jacket. He curled up on the ground and put it under his head for a pillow.

"Sleep," he said.

"Didn't you get any last night?" Ruth was thinking of the way he'd slept on the bus.

But Howard only grunted.

Ruth took a few swigs from her juice box, then walked over to a big boulder and lay back against it. She closed her eyes.

• • •

"Took you long enough."

Ruth heard the words as though in a dream. She sat up quickly and looked around, squinting a little. The sun was now bright. Had she fallen asleep?

"Check this out."

Ruth looked around, startled. Who was speaking to her? She stood up. Howard was still fast asleep.

It was a familiar voice, but she couldn't see anyone. She turned to the water and . . . her heart did a double backflip.

There he was! Rodney! He was sliding down the bare patch of wet slope leading to the water.

She watched in stunned surprise as he ran up to the top and then, holding out both arms to steady himself just as though he were surfing or riding a skateboard, slid down the slope again, stopping himself just before the water.

"Rodney!" Ruth's voice was croaky with surprise. "Is that you?"

He turned and eyed her up and down.

"No, it's Julius Caesar."

"Oh." Ruth gulped. She didn't know whether to cry or laugh. *He'd survived*. She wanted to run up and hug Rodney to make sure that she wasn't imagining him, but she held herself back. He might disappear into thin air if she moved.

"Do you have any idea what it was like being thrown into the water?"

"I'm so sorry, Rodney."

"I nearly drowned."

"How did you get out?"

He didn't answer but ran to the top of the bank again.

"This is the first time I could get back," Ruth called.

"Don't make excuses," he shouted.

Ruth bit her lip and watched anxiously as he started sliding down the slope. Any minute he might misjudge the distance and ... What if he ended up in the river again? That current was strong.

"So, what's up, Rodney?" Ruth asked.

"Call me *Rodin!*" Rodney said as he slid past.

"But it's not your name!"

"I've changed my name."

"But ..." Ruth didn't know why she found this so disconcerting. "Mary Ellen called you Rodney!"

He slid to a stop, walked up the bank, and stared at her.

"You can't just change it," Ruth persisted.

"Why not?"

"It might hurt her feelings."

"So?"

"Well ..." She felt foolish.

"Do you know of a law that says you can't change your name?"

Ruth tried to think. "No, I don't. Sorry I mentioned it."

"Oh, call me Rodney, then," the rat grumbled. "Everyone else does!"

"I've missed you," Ruth began.

The rat looked up at her. "I can't say I've missed *you* much," he said.

Ruth gulped and tried to look as if she didn't care; but, in fact, knowing he hadn't missed her was almost as bad as never having found him again.

"Well. Maybe I did a little. From time to time."

"Oh."

"But after the horror of nearly drowning"—his whiskers trembled—"I had to try to forget and build a whole new life."

"A whole new life?"

Ignoring her curiosity, Rodney got up, took off his boots, and started cleaning them with a stick. "You probably got sick of me sitting up there in your room anyway," he said.

Ruth would have liked to tell him that she had absolutely loved having him in her room, and that he was far more interesting than any human being she'd ever known, apart from her aunt, but she didn't know how to say any of that without sounding like she was sucking up.

"Things at home have gone from bad to worse since you left," she said morosely.

"In what way?" He seemed genuinely interested.

"Well, it's . . . a complete horror show now, you know."

"Do you *hate* them?" Rodney asked. "Your family, I mean?"

Ruth faltered a little. *Hate* was too strong, but when she remembered the scene that morning and all the other mornings, she felt weary at the very thought of trying to explain how she felt. It was exhausting living with her family, and she saw no signs of it getting any better in the near future.

"It's complicated," she said, "but I think maybe I was put in the wrong family."

"Uh-huh." The rat was staring at her; the long, spiky lashes around his eyes were lowered. "So how does *that* make you feel?"

"Like a fish out of water," Ruth said sourly.

"Go on," the rat said with an encouraging half smile.

But Ruth didn't know what else to say. She shrugged. "Since you left and Mary Ellen died, I'm a fish out of water."

"Be more specific!" Rodney ordered sharply. "And by the way, I didn't *leave*. I was thrown!"

So she told him about the way everything revolved around her brothers now, how selfish and spiteful Marcus could be and how wearisome and spoiled Paul was. She described the way her mother was always running late, always in a flap, and detailed the lack of order in their lives and the lack of money. As well as all the completely stupid things her parents got involved in, like inventions and art, when they should have been concentrating on normal things, like paying off the mortgage and fixing the house. The rat was, of course, familiar with most of it, and sympathetic too, but he listened intently with that same sneaky half smile on his face that made Ruth wonder what he was really thinking.

"Everything was better when you were around. So I came looking for you," Ruth concluded lamely. *Why was she telling all this to a rat? She must be crazy!*

Rodney brightened. He bounced up and down as though he couldn't contain himself.

"And what a good idea that was, Ruth Craze," he puffed pompously, and scratched his head as if there were a very big idea inside just waiting to be let out. "What a very good idea!" he muttered again. "What an *excellent* idea!"

"How do you mean?"

"You want to get away from them, right?"

"Do I ever!" Ruth sighed.

"And *that* is where I come in," he said, looking at her from under his sly, hooded eyes.

"What do you mean?" Ruth asked in bewilderment.

But the rat just chuckled. He stood up straight and gave her a mock salute. Then in about three swift movements he hopped onto a higher rock.

"It's no accident that you turned up here today," he said cheerfully. "I can see that now. So let's get cracking. We've got to get down to business."

10

"There is no real risk as long as you're careful," Rodney told her. "You'll have three chances to create your perfect life. If for some reason you don't like where you've ended up, you can return from each wish at the end of one day. If you choose to stay longer than one day, you'll stay in your new life forever."

Rodney was lying on his back with his front paws behind his head and his eyes half closed. "So . . . what do you say?"

The sun was still shining and the breeze was still making the leaves tremble, but Ruth felt as if she'd been catapulted into a different universe altogether. She'd just given the last of the biscuits and cheese to Rodney and watched as he ate them, stunned by how much he was able to put away. His belly was now huge and round.

"How will I . . . return?" She could hardly get the words out, she was that excited. Rodney had just offered her the most improbable but exciting deal of her life, but her cautious nature told her that there could well be a catch. She needed more time to think.

"Nothing to it." Rodney snapped his fingers. "But I'll tell you all about *that* later. First up, you've got to decide if you want to make use of this special offer."

"I think so," Ruth said slowly, "but I'm not *completely* sure."

"By all means have a think about it," Rodney said dreamily, as though half asleep.

They were quiet for a while. But Ruth could tell the rat wasn't asleep by the way his eyelids flickered.

"Could you go through it one more time?" Ruth asked, thinking she might have missed something important.

"Okay." Rodney yawned and sat up and tried not to look bored. Ruth noticed that he'd been in a distinctly better mood since the food. "You describe your perfect life and I'll do my very best to get it happening for you. My powers are limited, so I can't promise everything, but I can manage quite a lot."

"And I get three tries to get it right?"

"Correct." Rodney held up three claws. "Three bites at the cherry."

"And I can come back if I want to?"

"Yes. Before the end of the first day you may return to your present life through a red door, which will be provided."

"And will it be easy to find?"

"Very easy . . . Just make sure you know where it is as soon as you arrive."

"Do I need a key?"

"No keys." Rodney yawned again. "Easy to open and easy to close. If you decide *not* to stay, then you must walk back through that door by six o'clock. If you don't do that, then you will have elected to stay in your new life."

"Forever?" Ruth whispered.

"Forever." Rodney was getting impatient. "Now, we've been through all this already, Ruth. There are no tricks. No double-dealing. It's really very easy, and, if I may say so, you'd be mad not to take the opportunity. Not everyone gets this kind of chance to change their lot in life."

"Have other people done it?"

"So many that you couldn't count!" the rat chuckled.

"Do most of them stay?"

"I don't keep statistics!" he said shortly. "Look, I haven't got all day."

"Did my aunt ever . . . do this?"

Rodney shook his head impatiently. "I was able to help her in other ways."

"Such as?"

"Hmmm." Rodney gave a sly grin. "Let us just say there was a gentleman involved."

"Oh." Ruth sighed and tried to remember if her aunt had ever had a boyfriend.

"Was my aunt . . . in love with someone?"

"I don't have time to go over old news, Ruth." Rodney was tapping one paw on the ground. "Do you want to take up the offer or not?"

"When I come back . . ." She knew she was annoying him, but it couldn't be helped. She had to be clear about it all. "You'll be here?"

"*If* you come back after the first wish and after the second wish, I'll certainly be here to organize the next. But if you come back from the third one—in other words, if you choose to *squander* all your chances—then I shall bow out."

"Okay," Ruth said in a quiet voice.

There was a sudden movement from over near the tree and Ruth remembered Howard. She stood up and peered at him, but he was only turning over onto his side. How could she have forgotten him? She was amazed at herself.

"But what about Howard?"

The rat stared at the prone figure. "What about him?"

"Well, I can't just leave him!"

"Why not? He has to be the most unimpressive specimen I've seen in a long time. Where did you pick him up?"

"Rodney!" she said. "He's my friend from school!"

"He's your *friend*!" Rodney sighed sarcastically. "Well, we've all got *friends from school*, haven't we? That doesn't mean we consider them when we're making life-and-death decisions!"

Ruth gave him a hard look. "Well, I came here with him," she said. "In fact, it was his idea to come. He said you'd turn up, actually." She thought that might engender a little sympathy for Howard, but she was mistaken.

"Does it mean you have to go home with him?" The rat sniffed.

"Maybe not," she said. "But how will he get home?"

"He's got two legs, hasn't he?" The rat sighed as though it was all too boring. "Okay. I'll work something out. I'll make sure he gets home safely."

"Well . . ."

"You want to go ahead?"

"Okay. Let's do it."

Rodney sat up straight, suddenly very alert. "Have you thought about what family you'd like?"

"I've thought about nothing else for *ages*."

"Good!" The rat gave her a flashy smile. "So, what *would* you like?"

"For a start, I want my parents to pay some attention to *me* for a change. I don't want it to be all about my brothers *all* the time. And I want my parents to be *normal*!"

"Normal, huh?" Rodney was nodding carefully, as though committing all this to memory. "Can you be a little more specific about that?"

"I don't want new schemes or bizarre hobbies. I want parents who are happy to work in normal jobs and watch television at night and eat ordinary food . . . that they cook. I've had enough crappy take-out food to last me a lifetime. I want a house that isn't falling down. In fact, I'd like a really nice house where there is no chance of the tap falling off in your hand when you try to turn it, and where I can have a proper room with nice things in it." She was getting excited just thinking about it.

"So." Rodney hopped down from the rock and began walking back and forth on the grass, frowning hard, his paws clasped behind his back. "You want to be the center of attention. You want a flash house, and you want your parents to be *normal?*"

"Yes."

"It might be difficult getting the *normal* part right."

"Really?" Ruth was surprised. "I thought that would be the *easy* part."

"*Normal* is very close to *boring* on the scale I work with." Rodney scratched his head. "But we can try."

Ruth had a sudden flash from the previous week of her mother standing in the middle of the street with her arms held out. *Come on, Ruthie,* Mrs. Craze had called, *come and welcome the rain!* Ruth had seen at least three neighbors peering through their windows watching her.

"Boring is absolutely fine with me!" she said grimly.

"Okay, is that everything?" he asked.

Ruth closed her eyes and tried to think.

"I'd like some friends again," she said in a small voice. "I mean *girl*friends. Howard is good, but he's . . . sort of not who I want to hang out with all the time."

"Fair enough," Rodney said thoughtfully. "I'll do my best."

11

"Are you ready, Ruth?"

She was sitting cross-legged on the ground under the bridge. The rat was standing on a nearby log looking down at her.

"Yes." Ruth tried not to sound nervous. "I'm ready."

"Okay. Let's go!" Rodney closed his eyes. "Remember—up some steps and through a red door and you'll be there."

Ruth nodded and closed her eyes.

Rodney began a high-pitched hum, which changed after a minute into a low, thundery one.

Ruth began to feel slightly faint. The humming went on and on with nothing at all happening. She snuck a quick glance at the rat from under her lashes. Was he serious? Rodney was now raising both tiny arms and circling his paws. He suddenly let out a high-pitched squeak and brought them down.

A rush of air hit Ruth's eardrums. This was followed by a mighty roar that got louder and louder. Then it stopped abruptly.

All was quiet; the color and light began to shimmer and dim and then faded away into heavy blackness.

Even though her eyes were open, Ruth could see nothing. The blackness felt almost syrupy, as though she might be sitting in a pool of molasses. *Was she blind?*

Ever so gradually, light began to leak in, almost imperceptibly. Ruth blinked hard a few times, trying to make it happen more quickly, but it remained a slow trickle. Until at last she could see!

She was in a gloomy hallway, standing at the bottom of a long flight of old wooden stairs. There were no banisters and the stairs looked rickety and unsafe, but at the very top, only just visible, was a shiny red door.

Ruth looked around. There was no way out of this damp, horrible place except upward. Too late to back out now. She was going to have to take the risk. *One step at a time,* she told herself, *and don't look back.*

Up she went, the stairs swaying and rocking beneath her. She thought she might fall at any moment. *Don't look down.*

At last she reached the top. Even though she was on quite a flat little landing, she still didn't dare to look down, but reached for the brass handle of the red door, praying with all her might that it would open and let her through. When it did just that, she breathed a sigh of relief.

• • •

It was summertime, bright and warm and wonderful with a clear blue sky above. *What a relief!* Ruth looked around. She was standing on the edge of a big heart-shaped pool. The red door she had just come through was nowhere to be seen.

The water in the pool was sparkling in the brilliant sunlight. She looked down and saw with real pleasure that she was wearing a bright red bathing suit—the exact same red bathing suit, in fact, that she'd wanted last Christmas and didn't get!

So where was she? And why did it feel so familiar? Had she been here before?

When she finally figured it out, she had to laugh with amazement. She was in . . . her very own backyard, only everything was totally different. With all the scraggy bushes and piles of old timber and disused furniture gone, it was actually really big. No more rotting posts holding up the veranda. No peeling weatherboards. No football cleats and bikes and discarded backpacks lying about, either.

In fact, everything was clean and neat and perfect, and there was no rubbish anywhere. Not one thing was out of place. The house itself had been painted a nice bright white with deep red trim. The big backyard was as neat as a pin, surrounded on all sides by a very high, green, perfectly clipped hedge. The old fruit trees down near the back fence had gone. There were two long, perfectly manicured flower beds with a little path lined with rosebushes in the middle. It led down to the back gate.

The huge shed full to bursting with all her father's bizarre inventions and her mother's pottery studio had disappeared. In its place was a cute gazebo with towels and rubber pool toys hanging neatly on hooks.

Ruth's heart rate quickened with excitement and pleasure. Everything was so neat and ordered . . . it was all too much. Almost.

"Ruthie!" A voice sounding just like her mother's, only softer and sweeter, came to her gently on the breeze.

Ruth peered around but couldn't see anyone. She walked around the pool, hoping like crazy it wasn't all going to fade away any minute. What if it was just a dream? How disappointed she would be if she woke up suddenly and she was back in her normal house! But the bricks beneath her feet were as hard as any bricks, and when she reached out to touch a rosebush, the leaves were shiny and thick. She bent to smell one of the blooms and smiled with delight, because the smell was heavy and strong. One of the thorns on the stem gave her finger a tiny prick, and when Ruth brought it up to her mouth, her blood tasted exactly the same too. She knew then that it wasn't all going to disappear.

"Mum?" she called tentatively.

"Over here, sweetie!"

A strange woman was coming around the side of the house with a watering can. The woman smiled and Ruth saw that it was her mother but that she . . . *looked totally different.* This mother was wearing makeup and high-heeled sandals, and her long gray hair had been cut off and colored with blond streaks. She was dressed in bright green three-quarter pants and a striped T-shirt, and she'd lost a lot of weight.

"Nice little snooze?" her new mother called brightly. "I'm going to fix lunch soon."

Ruth nodded and smiled back shyly. Something else was different about her mother. It wasn't just the new clothes and makeup, but Ruth couldn't work out what it was. Not that it really mattered too much, because this woman looked so wonderful compared to her old mother.

"Why don't I fix your hair so you can have a swim before lunch?" The new mother was walking over with a big smile plastered over her face. She reached Ruth and turned her around by the shoulders.

"My gorgeous girl," she murmured. "Such lovely hair."

Ruth tried not to feel awkward as her mother ran her fingers through her hair, eventually pulling it back into a ponytail, but . . . it *did* feel a bit weird. In fact, it took all of Ruth's willpower not to cringe when she felt sweet-smelling, warm breath on her neck. *Was this really her mother?*

Back in her old life, Ruth's mother hadn't done her hair in years, and she never called her *gorgeous girl.* Still . . . it might be something she could get used to!

"Think I'll have a swim now," she stammered, pulling away.

"That's a good idea." Mrs. Craze pulled Ruth back briefly and kissed her on the nose. "Then we can have lunch, okay, sweetie?"

"Okay."

"Enjoy!" Her new mother laughed gaily.

Ruth dived straight into the pool and plowed up and down for a while. It was quite a big pool and it took a bit of time to get from one end to the other. She swam a few laps and then began to swim around in circles. She knew she probably looked like a demented shark, but she really needed to release some energy and *take it all in.*

"How is it?"

Ruth looked over, alarmed to see that her mother was standing on the edge watching her swim, still with that same big, wide smile all over her face. When she caught Ruth's eye, she gave a fluttery wave with one hand—the long, bright nails flickered like lollipops in the sunshine. Back in her old life, her mother's hands were brown and worn and the nails were bitten right down.

"You need lessons, sweetie. Your style is all off."

"I know." Ruth turned onto her back self-consciously and floated with arms out wide, looking up at the blue sky for as long as she could. When she risked another glance, she saw with relief that her mother had moved inside. Through the large glass window she could see her moving around in the kitchen. Ruth was hungry, but she continued to tread water, trying to calm down and get used to the big change.

Eventually, she got tired and rested with her arms up on the side of the pool. She looked around the garden again, feeling insanely pleased. *Good old Rodney!* She smiled as she remembered the rat's instructions to find the red door first. As if she'd want to leave paradise! But maybe she should look around, just to be on the safe side.

There was a gate right at the end of the ordered garden. Would that be it? But no, it had to be red. Never mind. He said it would be easy to find, and anyway, in a couple of hours this whole new setup would seem normal and going back to that dreary old life would be the last thing on her mind. How lucky that she had found Rodney! Here she was in her very own pool on a hot summer day. Her mum was inside getting lunch, and she had on the new swimsuit she had wanted. What more could she ask for?

She got out of the pool and just as she was thinking that she would sit down on one of the recliner chairs nearby to dry off, her mother came flying out of the back door with two huge fluffy towels.

"Shower first, sweetie?" she said anxiously, pointing to an outdoor shower at one side of the gazebo.

"Okay." Ruth followed her over to the shower.

"Got to get that chlorine out of your hair." Mrs. Craze pulled Ruth under the nozzle and turned on the tap. "Temperature okay?"

"Yep. I can do it myself, though."

But her new mother insisted on rubbing in the shampoo and conditioner and making sure it was all rinsed out properly.

Ruth closed her eyes and tried not to mind the fussing. At last it was over, and she stepped out into the sunshine.

Her mother was holding out one of the fluffy towels. "Now, I've brought you your dress and sandals."

"Thanks." Ruth moved away a little and tried to take the towel.

"Darling," her mother said gently, "we can't have you dripping on the carpet, can we?"

So Ruth stood there while Mrs. Craze rubbed her hair dry and then knelt down to dry her legs and feet. She dried each toe carefully, as though Ruth were a little kid.

Ruth was on the point of saying *I've been drying myself for years!* but somehow the words stuck in her throat. Maybe she was still too nervous?

"Now put this on," her mother said, handing her a cute sundress, "and we'll have lunch."

Ruth slipped on the dress and turned for her mother to do up the zip. She longed suddenly for all her old friends to see her new circumstances. Lou would be so jealous of this little white sundress with the red trim, not to mention the garden and pool. None of them had a pool.

Ruth and her mother made their way into the house.

Once inside, Ruth simply stood there staring. Without all the piles of junk, the family room looked totally different. It was huge. Enormous floor-to-ceiling windows had been put in along its northern side, so light flooded in and there was a spectacular view out onto the beautifully manicured backyard. But the interior was something else. It had been elegantly decorated in cream and charcoal, with splashes of red in the cushions and curtains.

Above the breakfast bar was a banner that read *Happy Birthday, Ruth!* in fluttery gold lettering. *So! She'd arrived on her birthday. What luck!*

The door leading out to the hallway was festooned with matching red and gold streamers. Everything was tasteful and lovely, and there were three unopened packages sitting on the table.

"Are these for me?" A rush of glee made Ruth light-headed. One of the packages was slim and square and . . . She closed her eyes. *Could it be?* She was itching to open the package to see if it was the slim silver laptop she desperately wanted.

"Not yet, Ruthie!" Her mother laughed as she hurried over to the stove behind the breakfast bar and pulled a tray of freshly grilled hamburgers out from under the griller. "You must wait until Daddy arrives."

Daddy? Ruth winced at the word. She hadn't called her father *Daddy* since she was about six. *Never mind.* She'd get used to all this. She'd make sure she did.

"Perfect." Her mother was putting the meat onto the bread rolls. "Come and sit down."

"Okay," Ruth said. "Where are Marcus and Paul? Are they having lunch?"

But her mother was busy in the kitchen and didn't reply, so Ruth tried a different tack.

"The room looks nice."

"Doesn't it just!" her mother said, pulling out a chair. "Just sit down there. Daddy will be here soon."

The table had been formally set for three with table napkins. They both sat down to wait, the hot food sitting enticingly on the table in front of them.

Ruth could barely contain herself. She was starving.

"When will he be here?"

"Any minute."

Ruth gulped. The smell was making her mouth water like crazy.

"Could we start?" she asked in a small voice.

"Now, that wouldn't be very nice, would it?" Her mother wagged her finger playfully.

"But maybe he's been held up," Ruth said hopefully.

"So we wait," her mother said, frowning. "Now, don't fidget, darling."

Ruth had been mucking about with her knife to take her mind off how hungry she was, but she pulled her hand from the table and put it on her lap.

I could eat a horse and chase the jockey. She heard Marcus's voice in her head and suppressed a chuckle. He was always saying gross things like that.

She wondered again where the boys were, but before she could ask, her father walked in, whistling and carrying a smart new briefcase in one hand and some very colorful glossy brochures in the other.

"How are my two favorite girls?"

He was exactly the same, except fatter, and his hair was now jet black. The gray had gone completely.

"So you managed to get away, then, dear." Mrs. Craze was smiling frantically, as if she might be worried about something.

"I'm in charge now, remember?" Mr. Craze said with a jovial laugh. He kissed Mrs. Craze on the top of her head and then turned to Ruth. "Did you have a swim, Ruthie?"

"Yes," Ruth answered carefully.

"Did you enjoy it?" Her father sat down opposite her.

"Yes," Ruth said with a smile. "It was great."

"Her style needs work." Mrs. Craze's expression was suddenly grim as she leaned across to serve Mr. Craze some food. "Time we got her some private lessons, dear."

"Really?" He frowned. "But the Crazes are excellent swimmers."

They were? Ruth had never heard this before. But she was too hungry to care. She looked from one parent to the other expectantly. *When could they start eating?*

"On a more positive note," her mother gushed, "doesn't Ruth look nice?"

"She certainly does," her father replied. "New dress?"

They prattled on as they salted their food and took sips of drink, but Ruth was so hungry she had no idea what they were talking about. Unable to hold back any longer, she picked up the burger in both hands and took one enormous bite, and then another. When she looked up, her parents were both staring at her and frowning.

"Oh, darling." Her mother looked stricken.

"You've forgotten your manners," her father said sternly.

"Sorry." Ruth flushed and put the burger down.

"Well," her father said dryly as he picked up his knife and fork, "you must be hungry."

"I am." Ruth's face was red. "Sorry."

She watched her father cut off a small, neat piece of meat, pop it into his mouth, and begin to chew slowly. Her mother did the same, and Ruth, feeling almost sick with holding back for so long, tried to follow suit. It was hard at first not to swallow quickly, but after the first couple of bites she got better at it.

They ate in silence for a while. Ruth gradually grew calmer. After all, there were bound to be new rules in her new life and it was probable that she would occasionally mess up. She'd get used to it all soon enough. Hadn't she always complained that things were way too lax at mealtimes? She had hated the way her brothers snatched and grabbed and burped and elbowed each other at the table. Learning proper manners would be part of her new life and she was going to . . . *embrace* it. She was. *Definitely.*

"You got the movies for Ruth's party, I take it?" Mrs. Craze asked her husband.

"Sure did." Mr. Craze reached into the briefcase he'd put down beside his chair and pulled out a couple of plastic DVD cases.

A party? Ruth felt a flicker of panic but was too nervous to ask any questions, the main one being *Who will come?*

Perhaps she had a whole lot of new friends that she hadn't met yet.

She turned the plastic cases over so she could see the movie titles. She'd heard of one but not the other. The idea of a party was playing havoc with her stomach. She felt queasy, as though the food she'd just eaten had morphed into a lump of granite inside her. She wasn't at all sure she'd be able to manage a party.

"That is the one you wanted, isn't it?" Mr. Craze asked. "The other I thought you might like."

"Oh, thanks," Ruth muttered, trying to smile. "Looks fantastic ...

"Could I have some more soft drink?" Ruth asked. Mrs. Craze turned and looked at her severely.

"Could I or *may* I?"

"May I?" Ruth said in a small voice.

"I'm not sure if that is a good idea, dear," her mother said softly. "You've got your party this afternoon, remember."

Ruth nodded as though she totally agreed, but *what did that have to do with having another drink?* She tried to smile, but she could feel the heat rising into her cheeks.

Her mother was smiling at her. "You don't want to overdo it now, do you?"

Ruth shook her head. "No."

They were both looking at her now, just as though she were a greedy little girl half her age who needed to be told how much she could eat.

Lunch over, her father folded up his brochures. "So, when does the party start?" he asked cheerfully.

Ruth looked at her mother, who was clearing the table, and tried to stay calm. It was just that her real father never took the slightest interest in parties. Come to think of it, Ruth couldn't remember there being a party at their house *ever*, so this was all still very new.

"Like some coffee, darling?" Mrs. Craze asked her husband.

"I'll have it in the study, thanks." He pushed his chair away from the table and smiled down at Ruth and ruffled her hair. "I've got some catch-up work to do. You have a lovely time with your friends, Ruthie, and I'll see you later for the birthday tea."

"Dad?" Ruth was determined to catch him before the opportunity slipped away or she lost her nerve. "What happened to all your inventions?"

Both her parents stopped and looked at her, puzzled frowns on their faces. Their polite smiles unnerved Ruth further, but she tried not to show it.

"What are you talking about, Ruth?" Her father frowned as though he were trying to remember something.

"You used to work on them all the time," Ruth went on gamely.

"Oh, *that*!" Her father gave a dismissive wave and laughed. "I gave up that rubbish ages ago! It wasn't getting me anywhere. It was costing money, not making us any. I finally got sensible."

"What about you, Mum?" Ruth said tentatively. "Are you still making pots?"

Mrs. Craze threw back her head and laughed heartily, except

that it didn't sound like a real laugh. "Goodness me, no!" she said. "That time was so long ago I can hardly remember it!"

"And the boys?"

The smiles suddenly disappeared. They were both staring at her in a hard way, as though they were challenging her to go on.

"*Who*?" her mother said coldly.

"My brothers?" Ruth whispered.

For a few moments there was a heavy silence. Her parents continued to stare at her stonily. Ruth knew that she'd said the wrong thing and part of her wanted to backtrack, but somehow she couldn't. Then something quite weird happened. Mr. and Mrs. Craze turned to each other and began to laugh.

"Oh my goodness!" Mr. Craze had to get his hankie out to wipe his eyes.

"Oh, isn't she sweet!"

"Bringing them up!"

"Hilarious!"

Ruth tried to smile because they were finding it so funny.

"You are a funny one," Mrs. Craze chuckled, coming around and smoothing Ruth's hair out of her eyes.

Being up close to her new mother, Ruth could see what was different about her. There was no light in her eyes at all. She looked over at her father and a shiver of alarm ran through her because . . . his were the same. It was as if their eyes were made of something else. Something dead, like stone or . . . Her breath caught again. *Calm down, Ruth. Calm down.*

"Ruth, what is it?"

"Nothing."

"Your face has gone white, dear." Her mother's concerned, smiling face moved even closer. "Aren't you feeling well?"

"I'm fine." Ruth gulped. "Really, just a bit . . ."

"A bit what, dear?"

Embarrassed, Ruth shrugged and turned away. Their eyes were making her feel strange. But she couldn't say *that*.

Mrs. Craze took Ruth's arm. "What about a little rest before the others come over?"

Ruth couldn't remember the last time she'd had a rest in the middle of the day, but she let her mother help her up from the table. Maybe it would be nice to have some time on her own. She needed to calm down a bit and . . . get used to things.

"Yeah, maybe I'll have a read or something," she mumbled.

"Good idea." Mrs. Craze gripped her arm firmly. "Come on into the reading room."

The reading room? Mrs. Craze was leading her into the hallway. She pushed open the door to Paul's old room and Ruth stopped in the doorway and stared in wonder.

The room used to be full to bursting with her little brother's junk. All his toys were usually spread out over the floor, along with his clothes, his books, and his sports equipment. The curtains used to be torn and the wallpaper faded and peeling. Not one trace of any of that was left. An odd, flat feeling made her think for a moment that she might cry. It was as if her little brother had never existed! His room had been painted and redecorated with nice curtains and tasteful prints, making it look much bigger. One whole wall was now a bookcase and it was filled with books and CDs and expensive-looking vases and ornaments. There were a couple of easy chairs and a big cream sofa under the window that looked particularly inviting.

She didn't cry because . . . this was *exactly* what she wanted.

"Have a lie-down there." Her mother gently pushed Ruth toward the cream sofa.

Ruth did as she was told; she kicked off her sandals and lay down, resting her head on one of the big puffy cushions. She had never even sat on such a plush couch before. Lying there made her feel like a queen. "I'll bring you over some magazines," her mother said, "then leave you alone."

"Okay, thanks, Mum."

Ruth took the magazines. *Vogue*, *Harper's*, *Hello!* Imagine if all her old friends could see her now! How envious would they be?

"See you in an hour, sweetie." Her mother smiled from the doorway. "You have a nice relax."

"Thanks, Mum."

Ruth picked the first magazine up off the pile. She flipped through the hot new looks for next autumn and a gossip article about an actress that she had never heard of and yawned. She picked up the next magazine and read about a society wedding in England with eight bridesmaids and all the men in kilts. After looking at every picture she put that one down too, and simply lay there trying to familiarize herself with her new life. How wonderful it was. How lovely this room was. Everything was in its place. Everything was perfect.

Ruth loved the huge blue-and-white planter in one corner filled with maidenhair fern, and the nifty little ceramic table with a polished wooden chess set on top. She yawned again, remembering how she used to occasionally play chess with Marcus. In spite of the age difference they were of equal ability, more or less. He won sometimes; other times she did. But he never seemed to mind too much when she won. In fact, he was always nice about it.

"You're pretty good, Ruthie," he'd say as he packed the pieces away. "For a girl," he'd add, just to tease her. Some guys would hate to be beaten by their little sister.

Ruth was beginning to feel drowsy. The warm sun was shining in through the window and she was feeling so comfortable. She looked over to the corner where Paul used to keep all his special stuff—the plastic figurines, the dragons and cars and superheroes, his video games and all his board games —and a pang of something that felt almost like sadness went through her. She closed her eyes.

She is wandering all alone in her new back garden. Along the paved paths and past the rows of roses. How lovely everything is! She goes past the swimming pool and the new gazebo, down toward the row of trees by the back fence. A strange little shed behind the trees is grabbing her attention. Funny that she didn't notice it before. Her curiosity grows as she gets nearer. Ruth takes a quick look at the house. She can see through the big glass windows that her mother is sitting on the couch, and she can hear the canned laughter from the television.

Ruth takes a deep breath and walks on down the path and behind the trees. Now that she is here among them, there seem to be so many more, and the shed is farther away than she thought. It is almost a forest.

As she gets nearer to the shed, she has an odd feeling of familiarity. Yet she knows that she has never seen it before. A slither of fear slides in under her rib cage. She turns back to where she's come from, but the house, the bright garden, and the sparkling pool seem so far away now. Will she be able to find her way back? Of course she will. Besides, curiosity is eating her alive.

Shadows from the branches overhead are falling on the

windows of the little shed. She creeps up to the window. At first she sees nothing. There is so much dust and grime on the glass. She pulls a hankie out of her pocket, wipes off the dirt, and peers in.

Someone is in there!

Ruth's heart beats quickly as she tries to summon her courage for another look. She wishes that it weren't so gloomy under the trees. Maybe if it were still bright and hot, she wouldn't feel so scared. And yet something is preventing her from turning back. She swallows and steps up to the window again. She stares in at two dark, blurry shapes; one short, the other much taller. Perhaps they are statues, but . . . of whom? Her eyes gradually adjust to the low light inside the shed, and the figures become clearer. The tall one is dressed in long shorts and a bright T-shirt; the shorter one has hair sticking out around his ears and that reminds her of . . . *Oh no!* A chill runs like an electric current up her spine. Here they are. Her brothers! Out in this gloomy little shed at the bottom of the garden. But what are they doing here?

Ruth shivers. They are facing each other, but they don't seem to be moving at all. A rush of terror overwhelms her. *What has she done?* She walks around the little shed, looking for the door—first one side and then around the corner to the other side—but finds none. She has never seen a building before with no doors. How did her brothers get inside?

She walks all the way around the shed again and finally sees that there *is* a door, a small red one high up on the wall. Luckily, there is a wooden fruit box nearby. Ruth drags it over, climbs up, and, reaching as high as she can, just manages to push the door open. Scrambling up onto the ledge is difficult because there are no footholds. She tries three times and scratches one knee badly before she succeeds. At last she is sitting on the ledge. She looks down.

With no dirty glass between them, she can see that Marcus is smiling, one arm extended toward Paul as though he's about to ruffle his little brother's hair. Paul is looking down at the little figurine he is holding in one hand. Ruth's heart softens.

"Hey, Paul!" she calls loudly. "What are you doing?" It's a silly question. She can see that they are just standing there. She calls out again. "Hey, you guys. It's me, Ruth." Neither brother moves. Maybe they can't hear her or—she shudders—what if they aren't real? "Marcus!" she calls desperately. "Hello!"

But neither of them gives any sign that they have heard.

Just as she is about to drop down into the shed, a sharp, shrill sound pierces the air. Is it a siren? She turns around. There it goes again, and again. *A siren or a bell?* She peers back through the trees to the house, which is farther away than ever. *Could the house be receding? Or is the backyard getting longer?* The house is now only a little dot in the distance. Ruth looks down at her brothers again and gets ready to jump, but the shrill ringing sound wakes her up.

She was back in the reading room, and although her heart was still pounding, she felt a wave of relief. Here she was, back in her perfect house. Seeing the boys in the shed had only been a dream.

"That will be the girls at the door, Ruthie," her mother called. "Why don't you go and welcome them?"

"Okay," Ruth called back. "Just be a minute."

It was only a dream! Wasn't it? But it had felt so real.

Another shrill ring of the doorbell jolted Ruth from her reverie.

"Ruthie!" An irritated note had entered her mother's voice. "Get the door, please."

"Okay. Coming!"

12

"Hey, birthday girl! Many happy returns!"

Ruth's mouth fell open in shock. They were all there—Lou and Bonnie, Katy and Susie—standing in a line on her doorstep, smiling and holding presents, looking for all the world as if they were her *friends*. Ruth hardly knew what to say. She'd told Rodney that she wanted friends, but she hadn't meant *the same ones*! It was overwhelming. Not only that, but they all looked so happy to see her!

"These are for you."

Her mother looked on with a huge smile as Ruth opened all their presents. Lou had given her a lovely pair of silver earrings in the shape of ballet slippers. Katy had given her a pack of eye shadows—every possible color. Bonnie's gift was a gaudy pink-and-black fun cushion that said *Just try sitting on me!* That made them all laugh. And Susie had given her a gift certificate for horseback riding lessons.

"Thanks so much," Ruth said shyly. "It's really great you could all come."

"Wouldn't miss it!" said Lou.

"What about getting this party started?" Mrs. Craze said gaily. "What would you girls like to drink? The DVD is all set up and ready to go."

Ruth stood back as Mrs. Craze fussed over the drink choices.

"Now, you all just make yourselves at home," she called on her way out of the room.

Ruth looked after her mother wonderingly. In her wildest dreams she could never have imagined either of her parents behaving like this!

It turned out that everyone except Lou and Ruth had seen the film already, but it didn't matter. The rest of them didn't mind seeing it again.

"Could we go for a swim afterward?" Lou asked.

"Sure." Ruth grinned. She wasn't used to having Lou deferring to her, and it felt pretty good.

The front room had been specifically set up as a mini-theater. A screen covered half the wall. Heavy drapes hung across the windows. So where had the broken sports equipment, the battered piano, the table extensions, and all the rest of it gone? Ruth looked around in amazement.

"This is sooo cool," Lou muttered, plonking herself down in one of the deep leather chairs. "I wish we had a screening room at home!"

The other girls sighed in agreement as they followed suit.

· · ·

They spent the next couple of hours watching a DVD about a pack of stupid teenage girls in an American high school who snipe and whine and pinch one another's boyfriends. Ruth's friends giggled and yelled out comments and hooted with laughter in all the right places. Ruth played along, but she was using the time to settle herself into her new life. *How good is this?* she kept reminding herself. The tedious film didn't matter in the least. What did matter was that she was sitting there with all her old mates. School was going to be different from now on. She had friends again. *And* the family had plenty of money now. *And* her mother looked normal. She tried not to think about her brothers. If they didn't exist in this world, did they exist anywhere?

"How about an ice cream, girls? Or another Coke?"

Ruth's mum was so attentive throughout the whole afternoon that Ruth had trouble believing it really was her mother. First she came in to check that the curtains were fully closed, then to see if the sound was up high enough, and then it was a procession of snacks and drinks. Ruth had never eaten so much junk food in her life.

When the movie was over at last, they wandered out into the family room, where Mrs. Craze was sitting down in front of the television watching a show about football—something she would never have done in Ruth's old life.

"How was it, girls?"

"Great!" everyone exclaimed.

"Ruthie?" Mrs. Craze teased in her new, soft voice. "Did you like it?"

"Yep, it was ... good," Ruth lied, because they were all looking at her. "Awesome."

"So, what about a swim?" Mrs. Craze asked, pointing to a pile of neatly stacked towels. "Just take one of those on your way out."

"Thanks, Mrs. Craze!" Bonnie, Lou, Susie, and Katy chorused.

Ruth breathed a secret sigh of relief as she slid open the back door and motioned her friends through.

"What about bathing suits?" Bonnie asked.

"I think I've got some old ones," Ruth said. "You can wear them if you like."

"As if she'd fit into your swimsuit!" Lou sneered. "Bonnie is twice your size."

Bonnie's cheeks flamed with humiliation.

"You *are* putting on weight, Bon," Katy said lightly.

"I know," Bonnie mumbled miserably.

"You shouldn't have been eating those chips before," Katy added.

"Or the soda. It's so bad for you, Bonnie," Susie said primly.

So now it was Bonnie's turn! The heat was off Ruth. Lou and she were *best friends* again. So why didn't she feel more pleased?

Dressed in her new red swimsuit, she looked out over the

perfect back garden. The shimmering pool was still bright in the fading light. Her friends were splashing around, and there was a delicious smell of barbecued meat. Her father was flipping over the chicken breasts and sausages, and her mother was setting a little table with outdoor cutlery and bottles of soda.

All around her there was the idle chatter and laughter of people having fun.

Ruth looked down at her watch. Five minutes to six o'clock! She had to decide right that minute whether she wanted to stay in this new life forever.

But what was there to decide? *Of course she had to stay.* She'd gotten exactly what she wanted, more or less. Everything had been so ordered and so nice. There were things to look forward to and nothing to worry about. Her father was now the boss at work, so there would be more than enough money, and just think about all the lovely clothes she'd be able to buy! If not today, then some other day. She was now the center of attention in a normal family, just as she had asked. No more boring sports matches and tedious concerts or loud, raucous arguments about whose turn it was in the bathroom.

But her eyes were drawn past it all to the shadowy clump of trees screening most of the back fence, and the strange dream she'd had earlier in the afternoon came back to her.

"Come on in, Ruth!" Lou was standing in the middle of the pool holding a big plastic ball. "Come in and be on my team!"

All the unpleasantness of the past had been forgotten. Three of her friends were looking up at her from the water, smiling, waiting for her to join in. Bonnie was sitting on the side dabbling her feet in the water, still dressed in her shorts and top.

Ruth stared into the sparkling water. This would be the first of many pool parties. From now on, life was going to be full of all kinds of fun things.

"Come on!" Lou shouted from the water. "What are you waiting for?"

Ruth tried to smile at her old adversary. *But I don't like them.* The words flew into her head as though on the breeze. *I don't like them at all.*

Just then, Mrs. Craze came out the back door holding an enormous pink cake with twelve lighted candles and began to sing "Happy Birthday."

The other girls pulled themselves out of the pool squealing with delight and joined in loudly.

". . . Happy birthday, dear Ruth! Happy birthday to you!" They walked around the pool toward her, smiling as they sang.

Ruth stood transfixed. Why did they all look so strange? *And wrong.* Maybe it was that bland, sugary smile on her mother's face or her father's dyed hair. Maybe it was poor, silly Bonnie's fake good cheer or the glint of jealousy in Lou's eyes. Nothing was clear to Ruth except that suddenly she didn't want to be there.

Something lying dormant inside her had come alive. No. She didn't want to stay. *No, no, no . . .* Not in a million years! *Why? And why had it taken her all day to realize it?*

She looked at her watch and saw with dismay that she had less than a minute to make her escape. Rodney had promised that it would be easy . . . provided she found the red door as soon as she arrived. What a fool not to have found it earlier! What if she missed her chance to get back?

The dream was the only thing she had to go on. If she snuck up there through the trees, would she find that shed with the little red door? Would she be able to look in the window?

Ruth began to run.

She ran past the pool, along the paving stones, and onto the lawn toward the clump of trees along the back fence. *Imagine living every day with parents who insist on knowing everything about you! Who treat you like their little pet poodle! Imagine summer after summer of pool parties with Lou and the rest of them picking on Bonnie!* She would rather be back with the mess and the chaos of her brothers, with her fat, messy, loud mother and eccentric father, than stay another five minutes with all those *dead eyes . . .*

Ruth had the strange feeling that she was running for her life, and that gave her an edge she never knew she had. It felt almost as though someone had given her wings. She wasn't thinking or feeling anything; she was *flying*. And yet it seemed like such a long way. Perhaps some terrible trick was being played on her? Or . . . perhaps she was still in the dream and would never get out.

Her chest was hurting badly and she was almost out of breath. On she ran. What if the dream had only been a *dream*? What if that funny door was just a figment of her unconscious? What if the door was there but the fruit box was gone . . .

"Ruth, where are you going?" Faraway voices crowded into her head. "Come back, Ruth!"

"Ruth, come and cut your beautiful birthday cake."

"We're about to eat."

Her friends had dropped their towels and started running after her.

Ruth reached the trees, and when she saw the little shed she cried out with relief. She ran around to the far side. The fruit box was exactly where she'd left it in the dream. She clambered up the wall and this time she got up on the first go, just as her friends crashed through the trees behind her.

Ruth looked at her watch. *Fifteen seconds to go!*

"Ruth!"

"*Where has she gone?*"

Bonnie was the first to catch sight of her. "There she is!" she yelled, pointing up excitedly.

"What are you doing up there?" Lou called. "We're about to have the cake!"

Mr. and Mrs. Craze appeared and pushed their way impatiently to the front of the little group standing below Ruth.

"You have guests!" her father shouted. "Come back down this instant!"

"We've given you everything," her mother wailed, "and you repay us with *this*!"

"Don't go through that door!" her father commanded, and reached for her leg.

Ruth only just managed to jerk away.

She took a last look down into his blank eyes, at the perfect backyard through the trees, at the swimming pool and the rosebushes and the manicured lawn. She looked at her perfect parents and her perfect friends and put her hand on the doorknob and pushed it with all her might.

The door opened easily, and without even looking to see where she was headed, Ruth used every last bit of energy to throw herself through that doorway. Way behind her she heard the ripping sound of the new swimsuit tearing and then some loud yells and curses, but, terrified and exhilarated, she knew that she had escaped.

Down she went at breakneck speed through dark, sticky, damp air. She could see nothing and hear nothing, but prayed that Rodney had thought to remember some kind of parachute, or at least something to soften her fall at the end. Down, down, down she went through murky blackness.

13

With a loud *whoosh* and a thud, Ruth landed heavily on a muddy patch of earth right alongside the river. Heart racing from her close escape, she picked herself up and looked around. Never had she been so pleased to see such ordinary things! There was the bridge and the road, cows were in the paddock opposite, and, although it was cool, the sun was out.

She smiled in astonishment. Everything was just as she'd left it. Even Howard was still asleep near the tree. It was as though no time had passed at all. But where was Rodney? Boy, didn't he get it wrong! Well, they both did, actually.

There was no sign of the rat. No sign of him at all.

"I wonder if all normal families are like that," Ruth said aloud as she sat down on a rock to wait for him. A noise behind her made her turn around. Howard was sitting up and rubbing his eyes.

"Talking to yourself is the first sign of madness." He grinned across at Ruth.

She smiled back.

Howard stood up and stretched. He wandered over and took a swig from his juice box.

Ruth watched him, wondering how to go about telling him what had happened while he'd been asleep.

"I like this place," he mumbled, looking around. "I'm going to come back here."

"Yeah," Ruth agreed. "It's cool."

"I think I'll go up the river a bit," he said suddenly. "You want to come?"

But Ruth was thinking of Rodney. She still had two wishes left to get it right.

"I'll stay here."

He gave her a hard look. "How come?"

"I'm waiting for . . . something."

"Rodney?"

Ruth nodded and laughed at herself. It had probably all been some kind of dream, but she couldn't shake the feeling that Rodney would be back. Howard took a roll of fishing line out of his pocket.

"I'm going to see if I can catch a fish."

"You haven't got a hook."

Howard dug around in the other pocket and pulled out a rusty, bent nail.

"You'll need bait," Ruth said awkwardly. She really didn't want him to go, in case something happened to her.

"I'll dig up some worms."

Ruth must have looked skeptical because he added proudly, "I've done it before."

"Really?"

"When I lived with my mum, we used to go fishing all the time."

"Fishing?" Ruth stared at him. "With your mum?"

"Yep," Howard said with a smile. "She was really good at it."

Ruth watched him walking toward the bridge, feeling a little bereft. Maybe she should forget all about Rodney's promises and go with him.

But as soon as Howard had disappeared under the bridge, she heard the telltale scratching followed by a couple of polite coughs that told her Rodney was nearby. She turned, and there he was, standing on a rock some distance away, scratching his armpit and eyeing her carefully.

"Hello," Ruth said.

"I thought that *friend* of yours would never leave!" He sniffed.

"Where were you hiding?" she asked.

"Never mind." Rodney sighed, and then looked at her slyly from under his lashes before jumping down off the rock and leaning back against it. "Well, now," he said. "The last placement didn't quite work out, I take it?"

"It was terrible," Ruth said in a quiet voice.

"You said you wanted a normal family," he countered defensively.

"I know," Ruth agreed.

"I did my best!"

"I didn't realize my brothers were going to be *erased*."

"You wanted to be rid of them! What was I supposed to do?"

"Just because they drive me nuts doesn't mean I wanted anything *bad* to happen to them," Ruth tried to explain.

"Nothing *bad* did happen to them!" Rodney huffed. "I don't *do* gruesome."

"But it *was* gruesome!" Ruth grimaced, remembering her dream of Marcus and Paul in the shed.

"I don't always get everything right," the rat said angrily, "but I certainly do not actually *hurt* people."

"Well, what happened to them, then?"

"There was no pain involved. No fear, no distress. They were simply put *on hold*."

"*On hold*." Ruth frowned. "That doesn't sound like much fun."

"I wasn't aware that your brothers' *fun quotient* was part of my mission statement!"

"Okay." Ruth looked away glumly. "And what about the red door? You said it would be easy to find!"

"You're here, aren't you?" Rodney muttered, shrugging her off. "So . . . do you want to have another try?" he asked, kicking the ground and looking bored. "Or not?"

"I'm not sure." Ruth sighed. "It got pretty hairy back there."

"Well, I haven't got all day," the rat snapped. "Do you want to or don't you?"

Ruth got up and walked to the edge of the river, trying to think. *Would she dare do it again? No. It would be too crazy!* But a little voice at the back of her mind was saying, *Have another go! You don't want to go home, do you?* If she gave it another try, it didn't have to be a disaster like last time. She knew more now. She would give Rodney clearer instructions. First off, she had to find the red door; and second, she had to make sure not to get so overwhelmed at the beginning, like last time. She had to keep her head clear and bide her time for a while before she made any judgments.

"I don't want anything at all to happen to my family this time," she called to Rodney. "They're absolutely out of bounds."

"Done."

"So you won't touch them?"

"Absolutely not."

"And they'll definitely stay the same, just . . . without me?"

"Easy." The rat flicked one paw at her. "They won't feature in the operation at all."

"Okay. Then I *will* have another try."

Rodney looked animated for the first time since she'd arrived back. He scrambled onto the rock.

"So, Ruth, what kind of family do you want this time?"

She took a deep breath and tried very hard to keep a clear head. "I don't want *any* family this time," she said quietly.

Rodney raised one eyebrow. "What do you mean?"

"I want to be alone in the world." Ruth knew this sounded dramatic, but she'd thought it through.

"But *why?*" Rodney was incredulous.

"I've come to the conclusion that family life just doesn't suit me. It's too messy and loud, and you have to put up with other people's silly schemes, bad habits, and horrible ideas, and no one ever listens to you."

"Remember, there are some things I can't do," Rodney cut in suddenly. "I can't change your age, for instance."

"Okay."

"You're only eleven, so you're going to need a guardian."

"Okay, but . . . I want an ordered, quiet life. No family."

"Interesting." Rodney gave her a wry grin before turning his back. He hopped down from the rock and began to pace up and down with his paws clasped behind his back. "Just give me a few minutes. I'll have to have a hard think about this one."

14

It was freezing.

Ruth was kneeling in the middle of a row of other girls and it was terribly cold. She was starving too, but somehow being cold and hungry wasn't in the forefront of her mind. Surrounding her on all sides was the wonderful swelling and rumbling of organ music. She looked down at herself and with a pleasant jolt of surprise realized that she was in a school uniform. *Uniform.* She had always secretly longed to wear a uniform and now she was. *Good old Rodney!*

It was a navy serge tunic and blazer with a stiff white collar, a striped tie, and, what's more—she felt her head gingerly—a hat! (A rather hard felt hat with a badge on it.) She couldn't see her shoes, but they felt stiff and heavy. She had a moment of panic. What if they gave her blisters? She had never worn shoes that felt like this before.

Her stomach suddenly growled. She looked left and then right. There were about six girls on either side of her and a huge sea of them in front, all in neat rows, all dressed in the same uniform. She didn't dare turn to look behind because the whole mood was so formal and serious. Ruth felt a pang of excitement. She had no idea where she was or what exactly was happening, but it all felt very special. The girls next to her had their eyes closed and their hands clasped in front of them.

Ruth looked up. The gray stone walls went up forever on either side, with windows right at the top letting in the weak sunlight. But most of the light came from the rounded, dome-like space up front. Huge candles were dotted around on what looked like a stage, and above this was an enormous multi-colored stained-glass window. The big window was surrounded by a number of smaller ones. Each contained scenes of people draped in what looked like heavy scarves. There were women holding babies and huddling around looking mournful, and there were men in robes catching fish. At the top of the big window a man with a gray beard was sitting on a throne holding some kind of globe in one hand. *Was that God? Was He holding the world?* Ruth was fascinated. *What did it all mean?*

Heavy shafts of red and green and gold light poured down, giving the whole space a wonderful eerie glow. *Wow! It must be some kind of church.* It was like a different world altogether. She'd had no idea that they could be this big!

Auntie Faye used to go to church sometimes. If only she were here to answer a few questions. Then again, she went to an ordinary little wooden church, which, from the outside at least, did not look in any way like this one.

The girls around her were rising to their feet, so Ruth followed suit. Then they were singing, hundreds of sweet voices joining together in the most amazing harmony.

"Now thank we all our God, with heart and hands and voices."

Ruth wished she knew the words so she could join in. She was gradually losing herself in the music anyway. All those voices were filling the huge space with sound so rich and wonderful that it felt almost unreal. *Imagine this every day instead of crass male voices and burping and farting and arguing!* Not to mention that tuneless whistling her father did almost unconsciously. He told her that it helped him think!

"Who wondrous things has done, in Whom this world rejoices."

Ruth had forgotten how cold and hungry she was. The music was lifting her up, making her feel as if she weren't a body at all! She had the strong feeling that she was only a breath away from levitating. Never had music affected her like this. Part of her was already floating up to mingle with all that sound and light.

The singing continued and she craned forward. She could see an old man up front and guessed he must be the priest. He was dressed in thick, colorful robes with ornate decorations on the sides and he was singing too as he walked around in front of a big stone table on the raised platform. He was shaking some kind of gold cup on a chain. Smoke was coming out of it, and Ruth got a whiff of something musty and sweet. She couldn't make out his face, but she thought he must be very old because he was moving so slowly. Occasionally, he raised the beautiful clanking, smoking thing up high and bowed deeply. Each time he passed the shining gold cross on the middle of the table he bobbed right down on one knee, as if he were curtseying.

Ruth dared to look sideways down past the row of girls, first to the left and then to the right. She saw that the walls were lined with individual polished wooden seats and that in each one there was a woman dressed in a strange black-and-white costume with only her face visible. *Nuns! They must be nuns.* Before this she had only ever seen one or two nuns out in the street, and they had looked normal enough—in plain dresses, sometimes with funny little headscarves. *These* were like the nuns in the *Madeline* books. They were covered in long, voluminous black dresses and they had heavy beads and large crosses around their middles. Some of them were quite young. The stiff white stuff around their faces pointed out at odd angles like wings. She had never seen even one nun dressed like this before, much less so many together.

Ruth was intrigued. *Thank you, Rodney. You've pulled it off this time!*

Suddenly, she felt a sharp dig in her ribs. She turned to the girl next to her, stunned to be pulled so rudely out of her reverie.

"Move!" the girl hissed.

Ruth saw that the girls to the left of her had started to file out into the middle aisle and that by standing still she was holding up the line. The singing was still going on, but whatever had been happening up at that front table seemed to be over. Ruth got up and awkwardly turned to follow the girls as they made their way out. But when each girl reached the aisle she stopped to do a kind of curtsey before turning around and heading toward the back of the church. Ruth panicked momentarily. She had never curtseyed before. Should she try? Well, of course she had to. Out in the aisle she hesitated. *Which leg should she use?* But she stalled a moment too long. The girl behind sighed impatiently and Ruth lost her nerve. She made the mistake of trying to copy the girl who had come out from the row opposite. In the process she lost her balance, toppled over onto the patterned tiles, and hit her head against one of the pew ends. When she looked up, a sea of strange faces was staring down at her, waiting for her to get up.

"You all right?" The girl behind bent to grab Ruth's elbow and help her up, but Ruth could hear the mocking tone in her voice and pulled away. She scrambled to her feet; the sharp pain on the side of her head as she followed the row of girls out made everything around her suddenly seem very real. So much for the music! She wasn't hearing anything now. She could hardly even think. The gasps and titters from the other girls made her feel as if her head were filled with mush. She stumbled toward the back doors trying not to look as stupid as she felt.

Outside, it was bleak and windy. Clouds hung low and heavy in the sky. Ruth huddled down into her blazer, watching shyly as girls broke up from their rows into small groups as soon as they left the church. A few looked her over curiously before heading off either on their own or with friends.

The girls were around her age, although some were a little older, but there was no squealing or boisterous chatter, no calling out or *omigod*-ing. Not one girl was searching frantically for her cell phone, as far as Ruth could make out. She could hear the nuns still singing in the church and wished she were back there with them, more or less invisible and listening to that lovely music.

As the crowds of girls moved off quietly down a paved path toward a group of three-story sandstone buildings, Ruth followed. On either side of the path there were flower gardens, and along the high granite wall surrounding them, some big old trees. It didn't really correspond with Ruth's notion of a school, and yet all the girls were in uniform, so that was what it had to be. When she passed a group of older girls—all about thirteen or fourteen—the tittering and laughter became louder and she turned around. Mortified, she realized that they were laughing at her.

The girl who had been sitting next to her in church caught Ruth's eye. "New girl, are we?"

A collection of friends almost magically formed around the girl, and they moved to surround Ruth, all of them taller and older. "So what is your name?"

"Ruth."

"And are you a pauper or an orphan or . . . a miscreant?" the girl sneered. "Or all three?"

"I'm not sure."

"She's not sure!" the girl repeated. "Well, little Miss Goody Two-Shoes, have you got a mummy and a daddy? Or is Mummy a fast girl who likes sailors?"

Ruth had no idea what this meant, but the other girls seemed to. They held their hands over their mouths to hold back the sniggers.

"Is Daddy a sailor, sweetie?" The girl leaned over, lifted up Ruth's thick braid, and dropped it contemptuously. "Are you a little *accident*?"

"Girls!"

Ruth's tormenters immediately fell away.

The voice was not loud, but it had the tone of absolute authority. A tall nun had appeared seemingly from nowhere. She held up one hand to stop the tide of girls flowing down the path toward her. Everyone was immediately still and very quiet. Thick beads hung around the nun's waist, and a wooden cross was tucked into her leather belt. They rattled a little whenever she made the slightest movement.

There were perhaps fifty or sixty girls standing motionless now, waiting, faces expressionless. The nun clasped her hands slowly in front of her chest and peered over the heads of those girls at the front.

"And what is the rule about how we walk from Mass into breakfast?" she asked in a voice that was hardly more than a whisper.

Ruth's stomach churned. The woman had not even raised her voice and yet almost *because of this* she was way scarier than anyone shouting. Beyond the walls a car horn sounded, then two twittering birds swooped past. Someone called out a name. But in spite of these normal noises, the outside world seemed far away.

"Perhaps you can answer that question, Marcia?" The nun looked straight at the girl who'd been teasing Ruth.

"We should walk silently from Mass into breakfast, Sister," Marcia said.

"And why is that?"

"So that we might ponder the mystery that we have just witnessed, Sister," the girl replied without hesitation.

What? Ruth was intrigued in spite of her fear. What mystery did they just witness? Oh, if only she knew more!

"And what mystery is that, dear?"

"The mystery of Our Lord's sacrifice as commemorated in the Holy Mass, Sister."

Our Lord's sacrifice? What did that mean?

"And what were you doing, Marcia?" The nun's voice was getting lower and more threatening with each question. Her slimness and her height and her face—the long, perfectly shaped nose, arched eyebrows, high cheekbones, and full mouth—reminded Ruth of a fashion model but also—Ruth shuddered—of *a snake*. On a nature program, she'd once seen a snake silently raising its head, getting ready to strike a mouse. This frightening extraterrestrial being draped in black fabric with white starchy cardboard around her face was as beautiful and deadly as a snake.

"I was talking, Sister."

"You were talking." The nun breathed the words slowly and momentously, raising her chin, her blue eyes narrowing as she continued to stare at Marcia. "And you were laughing." She was almost inaudible now. "So tell me, Marcia, *why* were you talking and laughing, dear?"

"Sister, I was trying to make the new girl feel welcome, Sister."

Liar! Ruth wanted to shout. But there was a slight murmur of excitement among the crowd of girls. Marcia's tone was appropriately subservient, but it was obviously audacious of her to give any excuse at all.

"Were you, now?" The nun's eyes were like slits of blue porcelain, cold and hard.

"Yes, Sister."

"We'll talk about that further during recreation this afternoon," the nun said softly. "Be waiting outside my office at three thirty sharp."

"Yes, Sister," Marcia said.

"And bring a pen and exercise book."

"Yes, Sister."

So the nun didn't believe that girl! Ruth thought victoriously. But before she could get too pleased, the nun turned around slowly and fixed that blue stare on her. *Oh no.* Now the other girls were turning too, and Ruth wished the ground would open and swallow her. She had never been so frightened of anyone. Her knees were shaking. She suddenly knew what it was like to be that mouse, struck rigid with terror as the snake readied itself for the kill. The nun appraised her coolly for a few moments, from head to toe, as though she might be some kind of irksome insect.

"What is your name, child?"

"Ruth."

"I *beg* your pardon!" A flush of pink hit those high cheekbones.

Utterly confused, Ruth wondered what she had done wrong. She bit her lip and looked around for a clue as her own face began to burn and her legs got even wobblier. Perhaps the nun had been talking to someone else? But no, everyone was looking at her now, including the nun. They were all waiting, but ... *for what?* What had Ruth done wrong? She had no idea.

"Sister," a voice behind her whispered. "Say *Sister*."

Ruth didn't dare turn around to see who had spoken.

"My name is Ruth," she said in a small voice. "Sister," she added quietly.

"Let us start that from the beginning, shall we?" The nun flashed a cold smile for the benefit of the crowd, and the girls around tittered appreciatively. "What is your name?"

"Ruth, Sister." Ruth was close to tears. She almost never cried, yet here she was with that clamped feeling in her throat and a terrible prickling behind her eyes only half an hour into her new life.

"Well, Ruth, you do have a lot to learn." The nun's voice remained dangerously low. "You are clumsy and ill-mannered. I can only hope you are not completely ignorant as well. This being your first day, I will overlook your transgressions ... but remember, we have little patience here for insolence or sloth or uncouth behavior of any kind."

Ruth nodded mutely, a wave of blessed relief spreading through her. *She was forgiven.* She smiled tentatively at the terrifying creature in front of her to show how relieved and pleased and grateful she was to have been let off the hook. But something wasn't right. The nun was still staring at her ...

waiting. *What now?* Ruth looked around wildly. What was she meant to do now? Then she heard the soft voice behind her again.

"Say *Yes, Sister* and then *Sorry, Sister* and then *Thank you, Sister.*"

"Yes, Sister. Sorry, Sister," Ruth said breathlessly. "And thank you, Sister."

The nun gave the barest of nods and stalked off.

Everyone else followed silently.

Feeling as though she had only just avoided an execution, Ruth joined them. She was too scared now to look around, but she followed the crowd. Ruth Craze was known for her good manners. Teachers and other parents always commented on her politeness. And she was nimble and quick, not usually clumsy. *So what had happened?*

"Don't worry," said a voice at her side. "They're not all that bad."

Ruth turned to see a girl not much older than herself with dark, curly hair and blue eyes smiling at her. This must be the whispering savior. Ruth wanted to hug her.

"Really?"

"Oh yes. That was Sister Winifred. Wild Winnie the Wicked Witch." The girl laughed under her breath. "Or just *Winnie* for short. She's batty, as you probably gathered, but not so bad when you get to know her. I'm Bridie, by the way."

"I'm Ruth," Ruth whispered back.

"I know." Bridie giggled. "You told us."

"So are there nice ones?"

"Nuns, you mean?"

Ruth nodded.

"Yes, of course. They're not all fearsome. Come and I'll show you where to go next."

They turned a corner and continued after the other girls along a paved path toward the old sandstone buildings.

It's a jail, Ruth thought angrily. The great stone wall surrounding the buildings and the garden was so high that it had to be. *What did Rodney think he was doing?*

"What happens now?"

"Breakfast," Bridie said. "Then chores and then school."

"Chores?"

"I take it you're not a *lady* boarder?" Bridie looked Ruth over and grinned. "Sorry, but your uniform tells me that."

Ruth looked down at herself and realized for the first time that her uniform, although quite clean, was secondhand. The cuffs of the blazer were worn and there were some old stains on the tunic; her shoes were worn too.

"You're like me," Bridie explained. "We have to do work for our keep—just cleaning floors, washing dishes, and stuff like that. Nothing too drastic."

"Do we go to school too?" Ruth asked anxiously. She had a

sudden vision of herself down on her knees polishing floors all day.

"School? Oh, yes." Bridie looked uncomfortable. "Of course we do. Unfortunately."

They were now walking along an unlit stone corridor with a very high ceiling. Every now and again there were big plaster statues set on wooden pillars. One was of a woman with her arms outstretched and a blue veil over her head. Another was of a man with long hair. He also had his arms stretched out and he was dressed in a red robe. The weird thing about him was that he had his heart on the *outside* of his body, even though he was standing up and looked as if he was meant to be alive. Then there was another man in a brown robe holding a staff and a little child in one arm. This one had a halo of flowers on his head.

"Who are these people meant to be?" Ruth asked her new friend, slowing down so she could have a better look.

Bridie laughed. "You've got a lot to learn, haven't you? That one is the Sacred Heart. You must know him. That one is Our Lady of Fatima. That is Saint Anthony." She grinned at Ruth's puzzled expression. "You obviously didn't grow up with the One True Faith?"

"Er . . . no," Ruth said, "I guess I didn't."

"Don't worry, there are a few others like you." Bridie smiled. "It doesn't take long. Just a few months—then you can be baptized and you won't go to hell if you die."

"Hell?"

"Eternal damnation for anyone not baptized into the One True Faith. Which means being chucked into a fire forever. So best to learn quickly and get it done."

Ruth tried to imagine being tossed into a fire. *Forever.* "I think I was christened," she said in a small voice, hoping it was true. She could distinctly remember Auntie Faye telling them that Paul should be christened, but couldn't remember if he ever was. Neither of her parents was very interested in religion.

"Won't work," Bridie told her blithely. "It's got to be done in the One True Church." She pointed to another statue. "Over there is Saint Patrick."

Ruth must have looked perplexed, because Bridie took her arm and laughed. "Don't worry, they won't talk back! He converted Ireland. Everyone says he walks across the fishpond at midnight on the night of March sixteenth every year."

"Why March sixteenth?"

"It's the night before his feast day."

"Oh."

What on earth is a feast day? Ruth wanted to ask. *Do you kill a pig and dance around a fire or what?* But she kept her mouth shut because she didn't want to seem too stupid. This new friend Bridie might get sick of her, and then where would she be?

The corridor ended at last and they emerged into a small enclosed courtyard. Ruth smelled food and immediately felt hungrier than ever. The rest of the girls were going through some big wooden doors into what must be the dining room.

"You can sit with me if you like," Bridie whispered when they got inside, "but keep very quiet. Old Thunder Guts loves to pick on new kids."

Ruth nodded grimly.

The room was huge and lined with wooden paneling that reached halfway up the walls. There were about a dozen tables, each set with twelve places. The older girls seemed to be up at one end and the younger ones down at the other. At the front of the room was a hugely fat, ruddy-faced nun standing on a rostrum glaring around sternly as the girls walked in silently and stood by their places. *This must be the nun they call Thunder Guts,* Ruth thought.

"In the name of the Father and of the Son and of the Holy Ghost."

All the girls joined the nun in moving their hand from their forehead down to their chest, and then up to each shoulder, ending with both hands joined. Then they all said a short prayer together. Feeling very self-conscious, Ruth moved her mouth, pretending that she was saying it too. When it was over and they had done the thing with their hands again, the nun looked around very slowly from left to right.

"Good morning and God bless you, girls," she said in a rather gruff way, as though she meant exactly the opposite.

"Good morning, Sister, and God bless you," a hundred voices replied in unison.

"You may sit."

"Thank you, Sister," the girls all called back.

There was the sound of a hundred chairs being pulled out and then absolute silence except for the noise about a dozen older girls made as they came out of a side room and began to serve big dishes from trays onto each table. A dish of sausages came first and then a plate of bread and butter. The dish was passed to Ruth first and in spite of the fact that she was starving, she made the mistake of being polite and serving herself only one when she could have eaten five. She watched in dismay as the dish was passed around and everyone else served themselves two or three sausages until it reached the last girl, who took what was left. Ruth didn't make the same mistake with the jug of milk. When that was passed to her, she filled her glass up till it was almost brimming over, and when the bread came around, she took three pieces and put them on her side plate. She could feel the other girls at her table looking, but she was too afraid of her own hunger to care. Everyone was served now and yet still no one was eating! Ruth's stomach rumbled loudly.

"Is everyone served?" the nun finally called out.

"Yes, Sister!" the girls chorused.

"You may begin."

Everyone picked up their knife and fork and began to eat. Still no one spoke.

"We will be reading from the *Lives of the Saints* this morning," the nun declared in a loud, ponderous voice as she opened up a big leather-bound book. "The Feast of the Assumption is approaching, so we'd all do well to consider the life of Saint Teresa of Ávila."

At Ruth's table some of the girls rolled their eyes at each other. The girl at the end of the table with her back to the nun stuck her finger in her mouth as if she were gagging.

The nun's voice was dull and droning. No one seemed to be paying her much attention even though they were quiet. A couple of times she lost her place, and her voice became increasingly monotonous, almost as though she were talking in her sleep.

The girls wriggled about, giggled, and whispered little comments while they ate, but always with half an eye on Thunder Guts to see just how much they could get away with.

Once Ruth had partially satisfied her hunger by filling up on bread and milk she began to listen to the nun. The life of Saint Teresa of Ávila was actually quite interesting. Even a little inspiring. She had been a young girl with a mind of her own who refused to comply with the beliefs of her family and friends.

Eventually, the droning voice stopped. Ruth looked up to see that all the girls around the dining hall were staring at the nun, as if waiting for something to happen.

Very slowly the nun's heavy hand reached out for the little brass bell in front of her. One tiny tinkle and the room burst into life: a loud, gushing sound of female voices. All the pent-up talk and laughter came rushing out.

"Math exam today and I know nothing!"

"Jen Farrelly told her to pull her head in!"

"I'll rub her nose in it!"

Leftovers were brought around by the serving girls, but not enough. The three extra sausages that were brought to their table were snagged before Ruth could even indicate that she'd like one.

"So did your parents dump you?" a smiling redheaded girl opposite Ruth asked casually. "Or are they dead?"

"Ah, well . . ." Ruth tried to think. What would she tell people about why she was there? She should have worked it out before. Luckily, she was let off the hook by the girl down at the other end.

"Don't be so nosy, Tessa!" she exclaimed. "She might not know, and if she does, she'll tell you when she's ready."

"She's too young to have *done* anything," another girl observed.

The first girl grinned and pointedly looked Ruth up and down. "Not so sure about that!"

They all laughed, but not unkindly.

"What would I have to have done to get here?" Ruth asked shyly. She still felt self-conscious, but these girls seemed nice enough, and curiosity had gotten the better of her. The question made them all laugh again.

"Committed some crime," Bridie told Ruth in a quiet voice. "Instead of going to jail, the miscreants often get sent here."

Ruth thought back to Marcia's taunt earlier, *Are you a miscreant?* and filed it away in her brain. She liked learning new words.

"Remember Sadie Meehan?" The redheaded girl opposite Ruth looked around, and everyone else nodded and laughed.

"She stole fifty quid and she was only twelve!"

"What's a quid?" Ruth asked, wanting to join in their amusement.

Everyone at the table fell silent. The girl opposite eyed Ruth curiously.

"Are you having us on?"

"No. I've never heard the word *quid* before, that's all."

"So where *were* you before?" the redheaded girl asked.

Ruth decided the truth would do as well as anything else. "I was with my family."

"And you don't know what a quid is?" the girl said blankly.

"No."

"A quid. A pound. You know … money," the girl down at the other end of the table explained kindly.

"What happened to Sadie Meehan?" Ruth asked, desperate to change the subject.

The other girls smiled.

"Remember when she told Winnie where to go?" Their eyes lit up with the memory. "She didn't last long after that. They sent her to a reform school."

"So this isn't"—Ruth turned to Bridie and tried to keep her voice down—"*a reform school?*"

"Not exactly." Bridie looked around the table. "Most of us are here because our families can't have us or don't want us. See over there?" She pointed to three tables of older girls who were slightly separated from the rest. "That lot have been in trouble with the police, so instead of jail, the nuns take them in."

"What did they do?" Ruth was intrigued. *In trouble with the police! But they hardly looked much older than her!*

"All different things." Bridie laughed at her shocked expression. "Stealing, mainly, and running away."

Ruth was dumbfounded. *But they looked so ordinary!* Most of them had bright faces and ribbons in their hair and they were dressed in uniforms like everyone else.

"Some of them are tough," Bridie warned. "I'd stay out of their way if I were you."

"What about Marcia?" Ruth asked. "Is she one of them?"

This made the other girls at the table burst out into fresh snorts of laughter.

"She's over *there*." Bridie pointed to one of the tables just under the rostrum. "Those girls are *lady* boarders, which means they're being paid for by their parents. They aren't orphans or wards of the state. They don't have to do any work, and they get better food than the rest of us. They're snobs, and Marcia is the worst of them. Her father is really rich. He owns hotels and racehorses *and* he gives lots of money to the convent."

"Which means she sometimes gets away with murder?"

"Not with Winnie, though," said the girl at the end of the table, and the others nodded their heads.

"That's why we all secretly like Winnie," Bridie said, "even though she's nuts. She treats everyone the same."

15

After breakfast everyone went upstairs to brush their teeth and do their chores. Bridie was given the job of showing Ruth how to sweep the back stairs leading down to the music rooms. The stairs were outside and the wind was biting. Ruth's fingers were raw with the cold and almost numb as she tried to sweep the dust and grime away with a worn, wiry brush. Older girls were constantly running up and down on their way to music lessons, and Ruth had to stand aside to make way for them. Hardly any of them paid her the slightest attention. Often as not they stepped in her pile of dirt and she had to start again. She became anxious about finishing the task. If it wasn't the older girls, it was the wind blowing her neat little piles away. Bridie had shown her the front office where she must go to be assigned a class, but Ruth had already lost her bearings. How was she going to get back there? The big sandstone buildings all seemed the same. There were long, drafty corridors with enormous wooden doors and staircases leading . . . *where?* She dreaded finding herself in some place where she shouldn't be, face-to-face with the likes of Sister Winifred again. *And what about the red door?* Ruth knew she should find it as soon as possible but . . . right at this moment she felt too nervous to ask anyone.

Bridie had told her that a bell would ring when it was time to stop chores and get ready for class, but bells were constantly ringing and Ruth had no way of telling which one was which.

But just as her worry was turning into panic, Bridie, gasping for breath, ran back to collect her.

"I thought you might have trouble finding your way back!" she declared gaily, her friendly face alive with excitement. "But guess what? I've spoken to Winnie and she has agreed to have you in her class!"

Ruth was literally struck dumb, first with shock and then with terror.

"It's with me!" Bridie explained, wanting Ruth to be pleased too. "I'm in Winnie's class. She's not so bad when you get to know her. We'll be in class together!"

"But Bridie," Ruth said carefully, "she doesn't like me one little bit."

"Yes, she does!" Bridie laughed. "Don't worry about *her*. It'll be good."

Ruth had to smile. Bridie's easy warmth was infectious. "You actually went up and spoke to her?" Ruth was overwhelmed.

Imagine having the audacity to speak to such a fearsome creature!

Bridie grabbed Ruth's broom and dustpan. "Come on! Don't worry about this too much. Only the music kids come here most days, so you won't be checked by the sisters." She shoved the broom into a corner cupboard and reached into her pocket and pulled out a small leather-bound book. "Winnie gave me this to give to you."

"What is it?" Ruth took the book and stared at the gold cross on the front and then at the gilt-edged pages. The book wasn't new. There were worn patches on the cover, and the red page marker was a little grubby. Just inside the front cover was a list of five girls' names, none of which rang any bells for Ruth.

"Your missal," her new friend explained. "Everyone has to have one. You'll be in big trouble if you lose it. You must bring it to Mass with you every morning, and if you get some spare time in class, then you should read it."

"Really?" Ruth flicked through the pages. It seemed to be filled with short stories and prayers and black-and-white pictures, with an occasional one in lurid color. Ruth put the book in the pocket of her blazer and smiled at Bridie. She had so many questions, she didn't know where to start.

"So what class are we in?" Ruth asked.

"Seventh grade," Bridie replied. "Winnie said you could start there even though you're a little young."

Ruth was only in sixth grade. What if she couldn't keep up with the work? But somehow Bridie made her put all her apprehension aside, at least for the time being. "I don't know what I'd do without you," Ruth said sincerely. "I really don't."

"What are friends for?" Bridie said simply, putting her arm through Ruth's. "Better hurry now, or we'll be late."

The classroom was big and gloomy with about fifty wooden desks in rows. The ceiling was high and the windows were tall and had heavy wooden frames. Two lights hung down from the ceiling, but there was no heating. When Ruth and Bridie came in, quite a few girls were already sitting around in groups talking and laughing. Some of them stopped to look at Ruth curiously, but most were friendly.

"Heard you had a run-in with the witch this morning," someone joked. "Don't fret too much. You'll get used to her!"

"Happens to the best of us!" someone else called out.

A rush of gratitude for their friendliness washed through Ruth and she smiled. She was getting used to things; maybe this was going to be the life for her after all.

Bridie ushered Ruth down to the back of the classroom and opened up one of the old-fashioned desks, showing her the empty space for her books.

"Winnie said she'd sort you out with books at the end of the day," Bridie told her. "Until then you can share with me."

"Okay, thanks," Ruth mumbled, watching in amazement as a girl went around filling up the little wells in the tops of the desks from a big bottle of black ink. She noticed that some of the girls were holding old-fashioned fountain pens, which they filled up with ink as they chattered. The only place she'd seen them before was in a movie!

"What year is it?" Ruth asked Bridie bluntly.

A couple of girls at a nearby desk heard the question, and after glancing at each other they turned to look at Ruth curiously.

"You don't know what year it is?" Bridie was obviously puzzled too.

Ruth shook her head.

"It's 1951." Bridie smiled, but her eyes were skeptical. "What year did you think it was?"

But Ruth could only shrug. She sat down and opened the exercise book that Bridie gave her, trying not to appear shocked. She'd had the feeling something was strange but . . . this was truly weird. She wondered if Rodney had meant to do it or if he'd messed things up again. Maybe he'd forgotten to do something really important. Going back in time hadn't been mentioned, as far as she could remember. *1951!* That meant before television came to Australia. Before computers and freeways and cell phones and proper supermarkets. How was she going to cope without all of them?

There was a clacking sound of beads rattling. All the girls

immediately stiffened and went quiet as the sound became louder. Suddenly, the black form of Sister Winifred appeared in the doorway. Everyone stood to attention. *You could hear a pin drop.* Ruth now knew exactly what that phrase meant! She tried to make herself invisible by hiding behind the girl in front of her. The last thing in the world she wanted was another run-in with Sister Winifred!

"In the name of the Father and of the Son and of the Holy Ghost." Sister Winifred blessed herself, and the girls followed suit. Up to the forehead with the right hand and then to the lower chest, then to the left shoulder and then to the right. Bridie had shown Ruth how to do it and she had almost gotten the hang of it. Sister Winifred was standing on a little platform in front of them, her body turned to the big cross on the side wall, eyes closed and hands joined in silent prayer. The girls did exactly the same. Ruth looked around furtively as she tried to copy what everyone else was doing.

Suddenly, the nun called out, "O Jesus, through the most pure heart of Mary we offer You all our prayers, works, joys, and sufferings of this day ..." The prayer went on for some time and Ruth moved her mouth around pretending that she too was praying, all the while thinking it was crazy. She didn't believe for a minute that anyone was listening, especially not the poor man bleeding up there on that cross. But she was desperate not to call attention to herself in any way.

At the end the girls all muttered *Amen* and then they blessed themselves again. Sister Winifred opened her eyes and looked around. She stared down the row of girls and caught Ruth's eye for a brief moment. *Oh no! She'd seen her.*

"Good morning, girls, and God bless you."

"Good morning, Sister!" the girls chorused back. "God bless you, Sister!"

"Please welcome our new girl, Ruth."

There was a brief burst of clapping from the whole class, and some of the girls turned to smile at Ruth.

Sister Winifred nodded formally and said, "Welcome, Ruth."

"Thank you, Sister," Ruth said immediately, and then waited, heart in her mouth, for the nun's reaction. Had she done it right? Maybe she should have said something else, like *God bless you.*

But amazingly, and much to her relief, the nun was already turning to the pile of books on her desk.

"Be seated please, girls, and take out your notebooks."

The morning with Sister Winifred went by very quickly. Ruth had never enjoyed school so much. First there was religion, which was quite interesting because she had never known anything about it before. The first half hour was Bible study, with some early church history thrown in. All the other girls had their own Bible, and Ruth felt self-conscious because she was the only girl without one, until Bridie pushed hers over to the middle so she could share.

After Bible study there was half an hour of preparation for confirmation. The whole class was going to be confirmed by the local bishop the following month, and there was an astonishing amount of protocol to learn. They were told at what pace to walk, when to lower their eyes, when to look up, even how to kiss the bishop's ring!

Then, on the stroke of the bell, Sister Winifred stopped almost in mid-sentence and began to teach math. The same thing happened an hour later when she switched over to history. She was a good teacher, concise and clear and fast. She moved from one thing to the next without the usual messing around. Just a few questions to make sure the subject matter was understood and then it was on to the next bit. Up till now Ruth had found school too easy. Sure, it could be interesting, but it went too slowly for her. Here she had to concentrate to keep up, and she liked it.

To her immense delight, Ruth found that not only could she keep up with the seventh-grade work, but she also seemed to understand everything more quickly than anyone else. At one point she turned excitedly to Bridie, about to say how much she was enjoying it all, when she caught a glimpse of Bridie's work. She was amazed to see that her new friend was way behind with everything. Her math page was indecipherable and her writing was messy, with ink splotches and letters all over the place. It was like the work of a first grader just learning to write. And she was very slow. Bridie only managed to copy half of what was on the board in the time Ruth took to copy it all.

At one stage, Sister Winifred walked up and down the aisles to check their work. Ruth's heart almost stopped beating when the nun took a look over her shoulder. She had to fight the inclination to put her arm over her work and hide it.

"So you're not unintelligent," the nun said eventually, "but what odd handwriting!"

Ruth looked at the work of a couple of other girls nearby. Their writing was all connected up and hard to understand.

"Still, it's easy enough to read and that is the main thing," the nun said. She smiled at Ruth, who colored with pleasure. She had pleased Sister Winifred. What a feat!

"If you finish early, don't waste time," Sister Winifred said with another aloof smile. "Take out your missal."

"Yes, Sister!" Ruth said.

Unfortunately, Bridie's work didn't get the same reaction, but the nun was kind enough as she asked a few simple questions. Apart from her unintelligible scrawl, Bridie seemed bamboozled by much of what the nun had taught them that morning. After working out a time to meet after school for extra lessons, Sister Winifred moved on.

When the class was dismissed for the short morning break,

Ruth put her arm briefly around her new friend's shoulders.

"I can help you, Bridie," she said. "After school we'll go through it all."

"I'm too slow." Bridie sighed. "I can't learn anything."

"Everyone can learn," Ruth said firmly, "you just have to do it at your own pace."

"But I'm completely dumb."

"You're not dumb!" Ruth nudged her and smiled. "I know some dumb people, and they're not like you."

A sparkle appeared in Bridie's eyes.

"Really?"

"I know it."

Bridie sighed miserably, as though the weight of the world were on her shoulders. "Even if you could help me improve my writing, it would make such a difference," she said passionately.

"So Winnie is always at you?" Ruth asked sympathetically.

"Not Winnie." Bridie shook her head. "She's always kind and tries to help me."

"Who, then?"

Bridie looked at the big round clock striking half past eleven.

"Next class is spelling and dictation with Sister Gregory." Bridie shivered. "I dread Tuesdays and Thursdays so much because of her. She's the one we had at breakfast. Thunder Guts."

"So in what way is she awful?"

"You'll see."

16

"Bridie Fallan, which hand are you using?" Sister Gregory called loudly about fifteen minutes into class.

Bridie gave a low moan of despair.

"Sorry, Sister!" she said, eyes lowered. "I just . . . forgot."

Ruth looked over to see Bridie quickly change her pen from her left hand to her right.

"Forgot?"

"Yes, Sister."

"Well, then, we must help you remember! Out the front at once."

"Oh please, Sister, I won't do it again! I promise."

"Out the front, please!"

Shamefaced, Bridie clambered up from her desk and walked slowly to the front of the class.

The rest of the girls watched as enormous, blotchy-faced Sister Gregory pulled a grubby old piece of canvas out of her desk drawer. She grabbed Bridie's left hand, pushed it up behind her back, and tied it there by wrapping the canvas around her wrist and knotting the ends around the girl's neck.

Ruth was completely dumbfounded. What was going on?

"Well, doesn't Bridie look nice, girls!" the nun chortled, and turned Bridie around for the rest of the class to see. "Believe me, by the end of the year she won't even know that she has a left hand!"

This brought a titter of polite laughter from the class, but Ruth was pleased to see that the vast majority weren't impressed. Their sympathy was with Bridie, not the nun.

"Now, back to your seat, miss!" The nun gave Bridie a little jab in the back.

With downcast eyes, Bridie walked down the rows to her desk next to Ruth. She picked up her pen with her right hand and began to copy what was on the board. Ruth could see her lip trembling, but she waited until the nun's back was turned before she said anything.

"Why did she do that?"

"I'm left-handed."

"So?"

"All the other *left hands* learned to write with their right hand by the end of fourth grade," Bridie explained miserably. "I just never could do it properly."

"But why *should* you?"

Bridie stared back at Ruth blankly.

Ruth looked at Bridie's work and saw that the writing she'd done with her left hand was quite legible.

"Everyone has to learn to write with their right hand," Bridie said in a small voice. "It's just the way it is."

"No, it isn't," Ruth whispered angrily. "It's quite acceptable to be left-handed where I come from."

"Really?" Bridie asked skeptically. "Where *do* you come from?"

But Ruth didn't get a chance to explain anything because the nun had turned around to face the class again and was glaring at them.

"Homework, girls!"

There were sighs of resignation as they all opened their books.

When the class ended, Ruth got up along with everyone else. Her growling stomach told her that it was lunchtime.

Bridie was the only one not getting up.

"Aren't you coming to lunch?" Ruth whispered.

"I have to stay in lunchtimes," Bridie said without looking up, "if I'm in the brace."

"So when do you eat?"

"I don't," Bridie said grimly. "I hardly ever do when I have *her*." She flicked her gaze up to Thunder Guts, who was waiting at the door watching the other girls file out.

"Hurry up, girls!" the nun said loudly. "I need to lock this room."

"You need to fill your big greedy gut," Bridie said under her breath, and Ruth suppressed a chuckle. It was good to see she wasn't completely cowed.

"Is she going to lock you in?"

"Yes." Bridie nodded gloomily.

Ruth gulped, wondering how she could help Bridie. But she was starving.

"You're planning on staying too, are you, dear?" the nun called sarcastically. There was only Ruth and Bridie left in the room now. "Like to have your hand strapped up too, would you?"

"Er . . . no, Sister," Ruth replied, looking down at Bridie uncertainly.

"Get a move on, girl!"

"Go on!" Bridie whispered. "Go have lunch quick or she'll keep you in too."

"I'll try and save you something from lunch," Ruth whispered under her breath.

"Thanks!"

Ruth was almost at the door when she stopped. She looked back at the nun, who was packing books into a satchel. Such a horrible face! The eyes behind the glasses were so small and muddy, and her skin was so mottled. The red blotches looked like some kind of weird map all over her face. And her bulky arms stretched the sleeves of her black habit as tightly as another skin.

Ruth glanced at Bridie, bent over her exercise book with her hand tied up behind her back. It just wasn't right!

"Excuse me, but left-handed people are born that way." The words tumbled out before she could think. "Sister," she added as an afterthought, because it was not her intention to be insolent.

"I beg your pardon?" the nun spluttered.

Ruth stepped closer. "Left-handed people can't help it," she said.

The huge nun stared at her.

Ruth had the sudden, odd feeling that this was her mother talking. How many times had Ruth been embarrassed by her mum speaking up in front of everyone? Now she was doing the same! But Ruth didn't feel brave like her mother. She felt terrified, but she continued. "If you let her write the way that comes naturally to her, then her writing would be so much better."

"Is that so?" The nun took a step toward Ruth, and then another.

It took all of Ruth's courage not to flinch and step back.

"So you know all about it, do you?" The woman was positively seething.

Ruth had a flash of inspiration. All morning she'd been hearing about God. She'd been praying to God and learning all about God's plan for the world and for everyone in it. *Please, God, this* and *Thank you, God, for that.* Ruth hadn't had any experience with God before. But if He *was* out there and if everything they said about Him was true, then why wouldn't He want left-handed people to be . . . *left-handed?* Wouldn't they be part of His plan too?

"Why would God make someone left-handed if He didn't intend them to be left-handed?" Ruth blurted out.

"I'll give you exactly what God intended!" Sister Gregory snarled, and smacked Ruth across the face. "How *dare* you question me!"

Ruth gasped and stepped back, holding her cheek; the nun stepped closer still and slapped her other cheek.

Ruth had been smacked only a couple of times in her life, and never like this. Sure, she'd been pushed around occasionally, stepped on and squashed a bit by her brothers over the years, but never actually hit. Not deliberately. Her face stung with the shock of it, and the pain. Tears came to her eyes. But she didn't cry, nor did she retreat even one step.

"You insolent brat!" the nun hissed. "I've a good mind to give you a whipping."

"Excuse me, Sister!" Bridie was standing.

"What do *you* want?" the nun roared.

"Ruth is new today, Sister," Bridie pleaded breathlessly. "She doesn't know—"

"Sit down!" the nun exploded, and turned to Ruth. "Never have I been treated to such willful, outrageous behavior from one so young! Never! How old are you?"

"Eleven," Ruth said, deliberately not adding *Sister*.

"*Sister!*" the woman screamed. "Have you been taught nothing? What is your name?"

"Ruth . . . Sister."

Sister Gregory stood there with both hands twitching.

She was going to hit her again. Ruth braced herself and tried not to flinch. But then she saw that the ugly old biddy was actually *bewildered*. No one had ever questioned her before and she was floundering a bit. The slap didn't come; the nun suddenly turned her back on Ruth, opened a drawer, and began fishing around for something, huffing and puffing as she did so. *A whip?* Ruth swallowed. She was afraid again. She thought of Howard and the red marks all over his body. Now she would know what that was like.

But when the nun turned around she was only holding a couple of books. Her expression had changed into an unpleasant smirk.

"We'll see what Reverend Mother has to say about you, miss!" she declared pompously, picking up her satchel. "Off you go. Wait outside her office. I'll be there shortly."

"Oh please, Sister!" Bridie was on her feet again. "Don't send her to Reverend Mother!"

"Sit *down*, Bridie Fallan, and be quiet!" the nun roared. "Or you will be accompanying this brat yourself!" Looking at Ruth, she pointed one of her fat red fingers at the door. "Off you go!"

"But I don't know where to go," Ruth said.

"What did you say?"

"I don't know where Reverend Mother's office is, Sister. I'm new."

"Then wait here," the nun growled. She was beside herself now and looked like an enormous lobster, crusty and red-faced. "No lunch for either of you!"

She grabbed Ruth's shoulder in a vise-like grip and pushed her into a seat in the front row. "Sit here and don't move. Don't speak or turn around. Just sit here and think about how you will explain yourself to Reverend Mother. I'm sure she will decide that you are much too good for this place! Barrytown will suit the likes of you better." The nun gave two short hoots of laughter and rolled off to the door on her broad black feet.

"Bridie Fallan, you must have five pages written by the end of lunch!" she called. "Or it's the same again for you tomorrow!"

"Yes, Sister!" Bridie stood as the nun marched out.

They heard her lock the door behind her.

Ruth sat still, staring in front of her. She couldn't quite work out what had happened. After a few moments she turned around. Poor Bridie was diligently bent over her work. Her left arm was still tied up behind her back. A fresh rush of anger swept through Ruth.

"What should we do?" she whispered urgently.

"Nothing we can do." Bridie looked up, and Ruth saw that she'd been crying. "I've been putting up with her all my life."

"How long have you been here?"

"I can't remember being anywhere else. My mother died when I was born."

Ruth got up and walked down the aisle to her friend. "I can help," she offered.

"No point." Bridie looked at the door. "She'll know. I'll have to do it." She went on writing the letters slowly and clumsily, and then added quietly, "I wish I was clever like you."

"She's just jealous," Ruth said angrily, "because you're so pretty and she's so ugly!"

Bridie laughed, but Ruth continued quite seriously, "Listen, Bridie, I'm going to help you every night after school from now on and you'll get much better."

Bridie shook her head sadly. "Reverend Mother will kick you out!"

"Kick me out where?"

"You heard her. Barrytown. It's for the real toughies." Bridie suddenly grinned. "But don't worry, you'll survive there because you're clever. I'll miss you, though." Bridie held out her hand. "I've only known you for half a day, Ruth, but you're already my best friend."

Ruth took Bridie's hand, not at all embarrassed by this disclosure, just sad that it looked like it was all going to end.

"I'm so glad I met you, Bridie!" she said.

Ruth left Bridie to get on with her writing and went to the window to think.

There had to be some way out of this.

Of course there is a way out, a little voice told her. *Think!* Ruth turned around to Bridie with a huge grin. It was so blindingly obvious! What had taken her so long?

"Stop, Bridie!" she said urgently. "Just *stop* doing it."

"But I have to get five pages done by the end of lunch."

"No, you don't," Ruth said excitedly. "How would you like to come and live with us?" she asked. "With me and my family? How would you like to go to a normal school where they won't make fun of you? You'll be able to write with your left hand and lots more good stuff. We'll get you your own little telephone that you can keep in your pocket. How would you like that?"

Bridie burst out laughing. "Are you mad?"

"No!" Ruth said. "My brother has one already. We'll both get one."

Still laughing, Bridie entered into the spirit of Ruth's plan.

"So, where is this place?"

"Never mind that," Ruth said, "I'll get you there. But I've got brothers. They're not always easy. And parents who are a bit crazy at times, but they'll be kind to you. What do you say? Do you think you'd like to come?"

"But . . . your family wouldn't want me." Bridie smiled wistfully. "They've got their own kids."

"That's where you're wrong," Ruth told her. "My family will take you in. In fact, they'll love you. I'm sure of it. Having you come to live with us is just the sort of bizarre thing they love."

Bridie put down her pen. "Are you serious?"

"Absolutely."

"But how do we get there?" Bridie whispered.

"First, we've got to get out of this room. And then we've got to find a red door."

"A red door?" Bridie shook her head. "I really like you, Ruth, but I'm beginning to think you might be a bit crazy. Why do you want to find a *red door*?"

"It will take too long to explain now," Ruth said anxiously. "Can you think where there might be one?"

Bridie shook her head again.

"Well, we're just going to have to look. First thing is to get out of this room before Thunder Guts gets back."

"But we're locked in!"

"How about the windows?" Ruth went to one of the old windows and unlocked the catch. Then, without any difficulty, she pulled up the sash. Smiling, she turned to Bridie. "Come on!"

Bridie stood still in the middle of the classroom.

"Just think of being free!" said Ruth. "You decide when and what you eat and when you sleep. You decide when and if you'll go to church or for a walk. You decide which hand you use for writing!"

Bridie stared at her for a moment and then she took a deep breath. "Will you help me take off this brace?" she said with a slow grin.

"Of course!"

Luckily, the classroom was on the ground floor. Still, it was quite a drop and Ruth scraped the backs of her thighs on the old, splintery wood. The rest of the girls were still in the dining room at lunch, so there was no one to see them. Once they were out and standing in the concrete playground, Ruth had a moment of misgiving. Maybe it was unfair to drag Bridie along. If they got caught, they would be in so much trouble. Then she remembered Bridie's hand being tied up in the sling. It was completely unfair that she should have to put up with six more years of old Thunder Guts.

"We'd better start looking for the red door."

"What will we say if we get caught?" Bridie asked timidly.

"Don't worry, I'll think of something." Ruth looked at Bridie's frightened face. "I just know we're going to find it. We've got time. We've got until six tonight."

The girls ran across the playground to the front gate, which was closed. Sticking close to the sandstone wall, they crept along it past the tennis courts and classrooms. There was plenty of cover for them to hide behind if they saw anyone, because there were trees and shrubs planted all along the edge of the wall.

"Someone *will* catch us," Bridie moaned, peering out from behind the shelter shed. "It's just a matter of time. You can't do anything secretly around here. By six o'clock tonight they'll be organizing our transfer to Barrytown."

"Not if we find the door," Ruth said. "Come on, Bridie, think!" She was already imagining Bridie sharing her bedroom at home. It would be like having a sister. How nice it would be not being the only girl in the family. "Does this wall go right around all the buildings?"

Bridie nodded. "It encloses the school, the convent, and the gardens."

"The convent?"

"That's where the nuns live. But we're not allowed anywhere near there. It's out of bounds to students."

"Okay, then let's start off in the school grounds."

"I'm pretty sure there are no red doors," Bridie said worriedly.

"One way or another it will be here." Ruth sounded surer than she felt. "It has to be."

But after going all around the perimeter of the school buildings without finding a red door, she too lost a little confidence. *What if Rodney mixed things up this time? What if he forgot to tell her something important?*

They ended up at the edge of the playground in front of a high wire fence. Behind the fence was a lovely green garden with lots of big trees. A gardener was kneeling, planting seedlings into a big bed of well-turned earth. On the other side of the garden was an ornate building attached to the bigger school building by a walkway on the first floor.

"From here on is the convent," Bridie said. "We can't go any farther."

"We've got to keep looking," Ruth said.

"But they'll catch us," Bridie whispered.

Behind them came the sudden noise of girls spilling out onto the playground from lunch. Ruth teetered on the edge of turning back. Then the memory of Sister Gregory's two hard slaps surfaced in her mind and she decided that now wasn't the time to give up.

"Let's do it," Ruth said through gritted teeth. "If we go back we'll get caught anyway. This is a chance for you to get away. Just think! That old bat won't be able to boss you around anymore. Or put your arm in that thing. We'll have so much fun together."

Bridie nodded without meeting Ruth's eyes.

"Okay."

They waited for the gardener to turn his back before pushing open the wire gate.

Once they were inside the convent grounds, they ran as fast as they could straight for the protection of the trees. Safely secluded behind an enormous fig tree, they looked about, trying to get a feel for where they should go next. All was very quiet compared with the school grounds. There were a few nuns about, but most of them were very old. They either shuffled along quietly praying or, with heads bowed, read from their little black books. Certainly none of them were on the lookout for a couple of wayward schoolgirls. Still, Ruth's heart was in her mouth. They were in forbidden territory, and she knew it would only take one of them to look up and call the alarm, and all would be lost.

Ruth pointed to another big tree almost directly outside the main entrance to the convent. "From there we'll be able to see right along to the corner."

Looking about first to make sure they were not being watched, they ran for the tree. They could see right into the magnificent front porch. The heavy, polished wood front door was closed. It was at least two and a half meters high and set into an even bigger delicately carved arch. All around the actual door were stained-glass depictions of saints and Bible scenes. A shining brass doorbell hung beside the door.

Bridie was staring at the door and a pained expression flitted across her face.

"What?" Ruth prodded her.

"I think I *do* remember a red door," Bridie said softly, "but I'm not sure."

"Where?" Ruth asked excitedly.

Bridie cupped her chin with both hands and frowned.

Ruth watched her in dismay. Bridie was looking into the distance with a dreamy expression on her face, as though she could see things that weren't even there.

"Do you remember where?" Ruth asked again, trying to be patient. *Come on, Bridie, now isn't the time to get all misty-eyed!*

Bridie's expression gradually lightened and she grabbed Ruth's hand and squeezed it. "Being here has brought it back," she whispered.

"What?" Ruth said breathlessly. "Tell me what you remember."

"I remember being very young," Bridie began, "maybe only three or four, and I was really sick. They took me in through that door." She pointed to the grand front entrance to the convent. "And up some stairs. I was put into a little room by myself, but I could see through the slats in the wall that there were about six beds next door, all with sick nuns in them. I was in a kind of hospital. I know it was inside that building.

"I was very little. It was strange seeing all the old nuns sitting up in bed without their veils on." She laughed. "They had these little white caps on their heads and..." She looked into the distance, her face screwed up into a frown as she tried to recall more.

Ruth nodded enthusiastically, but she was finding it

increasingly difficult to be patient. She wanted to know if Bridie remembered a red door. Childhood memories could wait. Horrible old Sister Gregory would have found the Reverend Mother by now. She might be taking her time getting back in order to make Ruth sweat a little more, but still . . . it wouldn't be long before she found out that her locked-up charges had made a run for it. And then . . . well, Ruth didn't really want to think about what might happen then!

"So what else do you remember?" she asked hopefully. *Come on, Bridie!*

"Sister Winifred brought a woman to see me." Bridie clutched Ruth's arm. "I remember her saying, 'Here she is, Jean.' The woman was young, and she was wearing a purple dress with small white spots and had a white straw hat. She knelt down next to me and wiped my forehead with a cloth—I must have had a temperature—and she kept saying, 'You've got to get better, darling.'" Bridie's voice faltered. "Sister said something like, 'She is going to live, Jean. Don't worry, she will live.'"

"Was the woman a doctor?" Ruth asked.

"My mother's name was Jean," Bridie whispered. "That is all I've ever been told about my mother. That her name was Jean."

"Oh."

Bridie turned to Ruth. "Thank you." The tears that had gathered in her eyes spilled over. "That memory was locked in my head," she explained.

"Okay," Ruth said, "that's good, but what about the red door?"

Bridie squinted, thinking hard, then gave Ruth a small delighted smile.

"There's an old, filled-in fireplace," she whispered excitedly, "in the same room as those sick nuns. I remember seeing it when I was well enough to leave the hospital. It's under a little ledge in the corner of the room. And right next to that ledge is a red door. I ... I can see it now."

They looked at each other and then back at the imposing front door.

"But how are we going to get in there?" Ruth muttered, staring at the closed door.

"I've got a friend who could help us get into the convent," Bridie said.

"Who?"

"She works in the laundry. She doesn't speak much English, but I know she'll help. There's a corridor that leads from the laundry into the convent. From there we'll just have to guess. I know it's on the top floor."

"Attention, girls! Would Ruth Craze and Bridie Fallan come to the office immediately!" Sister Gregory's voice barked over the loudspeaker. *"Ruth Craze and Bridie Fallan to the office at once!"*

"Come on." Bridie pulled Ruth up. "We haven't got much time!"

They ran back into the school grounds, through hordes

of girls sitting around playing cards and gossiping and then straight through a game of netball.

"Hey, off the court, you two!" someone protested.

"You're wanted in the office!" someone else yelled.

"We know," Bridie yelled back. "We're on our way!"

In through the front door, down past the senior classrooms, and out into the internal courtyard they ran. Ruth's heart dived when she saw two young nuns walking toward them.

"We're wanted, Sisters," Bridie called, not slowing down, "in the office."

"Oh." One nun's face registered the import of this. "You two are the girls who ..."

But the other nun was looking at them severely.

"You're heading the wrong way," she said.

Ruth's instinct was to stop and make some excuse, but Bridie pulled her on impatiently.

"Come on!"

They ran through another corridor and then out to the back of the school. All the buildings were shabbier. There was a sports equipment shed with a wire gate, but apart from an old man pushing a wheelbarrow, there was no one about.

Bridie led the way toward a building with steam and noise coming from its wide-open door. Ruth's eyes took a few moments to adjust, but once inside she saw that she was in the convent's laundry. The clunking noise was coming from two huge washing machines. At least a dozen washing baskets lined the walls. On one side they were loaded up with piles of clean white shirts; on the other, mountains of soiled ones.

Near the window, an old Chinese woman was working an industrial iron. She was wearing a dark dress covered with a big work apron, and her short, straight gray hair stood out from her head almost at right angles. When she saw Bridie, her face broke into a warm smile.

The old woman stopped what she was doing and held out her arms to Bridie. Her face was very round and red, there was sweat dripping from her forehead and patches of it under her arms, and her hands were as rough and big as a builder's.

"This is my friend Ling," Bridie explained, hugging the woman fiercely.

"My baby girl." The old woman laughed. She put a large hand to Bridie's neck and drew out from beneath her shirt a tiny gold dragon threaded onto a fine chain.

Bridie held it out for Ruth to see. "She gave me this when I was three."

"From China?" Ruth asked curiously. The old woman nodded and Ruth took a closer look. The work was very old and fine and it reminded her of . . . Rodney, in an odd way.

"It mean 'Good Luck.'" Ling smiled at Ruth through gold front teeth. "I have other good-luck charms too."

"Like what?" Ruth asked. *Like Rodney?*

"Ah!" Ling began to laugh.

"We have to get to the infirmary, Ling," Bridie said. "Can you show us?"

"Why you go there?" she asked after a pause, shaking her head.

"No time now." Bridie grabbed her arm. "*Please*, Ling."

"Okay." Ling laughed noiselessly. "But so bad…very naughty."

"I know, Ling."

Ling led them through the back of the laundry and then through another door. She opened it, stuck her head out for a quick look, and, seeing that the coast was clear, pushed them out into a lobby area and pointed them toward a staircase.

"There," she said. "Go up to top. Then across to where sisters live. From there more very thin stairs and at top you find sickroom."

"Thanks, Ling." Bridie kissed her.

They both ran for the staircase. It was made of polished, carved wood and was very wide. At the top there was a long, light-filled corridor.

They were halfway down the hallway when they heard voices. Two nuns came into view at the end.

"Quick." Bridie pulled Ruth behind the nearest pillar. They waited until the nuns' footsteps faded before venturing out again.

They made it to the end of the corridor without meeting

anyone else and came out onto a small landing with a flight of narrow stairs leading up. Suddenly, a shrill alarm went off and both girls jumped. It was just like a fire alarm and it didn't stop.

"That's the emergency bell," Bridie explained. "It means the whole school is on alert." She smiled nervously. "Everyone knows we're missing now."

"Never mind!" Ruth said gamely, but the shrill noise was terrifying. "So where to now?"

"I reckon the infirmary is up there." Bridie pointed to the narrow flight of stairs. "In fact, I'm sure of it."

But before they were even able to get to the first stair, a door silently slid open and there was . . . *Oh no!* Ruth gave an involuntary gasp. Sister Gregory!

Like an apparition she stood there, dark and ominous, as menacing as a giant, overfed crow. Ruth and Bridie stared back at her in shock.

For a big woman, Sister Gregory could move fast. She grabbed each girl tightly by one arm without even uttering a word. Her fingers were like steel rods. So it was over. Ruth's heart took an almighty dive. What terrible luck! They had been caught just before the finish line. *What would happen now? What was in store for them? More slaps? Whippings? If she was sent to Barrytown, she'd never get back home. And what about Bridie?*

A mysterious force sputtered to life in her chest and ran like electricity down her legs and into her arms, even into her fingers. She had no idea what it was or where it had come from, but suddenly she felt strong again. She knew with everything in her that she must not give in without a fight.

"Let go of me!" She twisted her body around sharply and kicked the nun in the shins with her heavy shoes. "Take your hands off me, you bully!"

To say that Sister Gregory was not used to being kicked was the understatement of the decade. In her shock she lost her grip on Ruth's arm. Ruth was free, but Bridie wasn't, and as far as Ruth was concerned, nothing was going to happen without her. She grabbed hold of Bridie's other arm and began to pull her away from the nun.

"Come on!" she yelled. "Fight her!"

Bridie seemed to find her inner force too, because she struggled hard. But although she was doing her best to get away, she couldn't break the nun's grip.

Ruth had an idea. With her free hand, she caught hold of Sister Gregory's headdress and tugged. First the outer veil pulled loose, and then the white, starched fabric around the nun's face came away, revealing stiff steel-gray hair cut close to her head. The nun was beside herself. Sobbing with rage and humiliation, Sister Gregory let Bridie go and clutched at her wimple.

Ruth took a last look at the disheveled nun and ran for the stairs.

"Come on!" she yelled.

But Bridie was rooted to the spot, staring at Sister Gregory in shock.

Ruth ran back, lunged for her hand, and pulled her up the stairs, three at a time. Sister Gregory, holding the bits and pieces of her wimple in one hand, wasn't far behind.

At the top was a dusty little landing. At first it seemed there was nothing else. Ruth looked around wildly. Behind them, the heavy footsteps of Thunder Guts were getting closer.

She looked helplessly at her friend. Maybe Bridie had imagined the whole thing. But Bridie rushed past her and pushed open a dark wood door that Ruth hadn't seen. They ran through into a strange world of white. White walls. Six white beds with white coverings. And in the beds, six old ladies in little white caps and identical white nightgowns.

A young nun dressed in a normal black habit but with a large white apron tied over the front was tending one of the old women. She turned and looked up when Ruth and Bridie entered the room and her mouth fell open.

"What in God's name!" she exclaimed in a thick Irish brogue, too surprised to be cross. "Is that you, Bridie Fallan? In the name of the Lord, what are you doing *here*?"

"Sorry, Sister Anne," Bridie said, gasping for breath. "Can you tell us where ... I've forgotten ... where that little red door is?"

The nun pointed to a corner of the room and, much to Ruth's relief, there it was: a small red door! To the side of the mantelpiece over the filled-in fireplace, just as Bridie had remembered. They grinned at each other in relief and made a dash for it just as the furious figure of Sister Gregory appeared in the doorway.

"Catch those girls, Sister Anne!" she bellowed.

All the old nuns sat up to see what was going on.

Ruth and Bridie were already at the red door.

"You first," Ruth yelled, opening the door. "Just jump. It'll be okay."

Bridie stared down into the darkness fearfully.

"But ... there's nothing there!" she wailed.

"I'll go first and show you."

Ruth held out a hand to Bridie. But then to her dismay Sister Gregory appeared behind her friend.

"Quick, grab my hand and we'll go together!"

Ruth managed to clutch one of Bridie's hands, but Bridie couldn't move because Sister Gregory was pulling her the other way.

"Let her go," Ruth screamed, "you great stinking bully!"

But Sister Gregory had no intention of letting go. She might have lost the battle, but she was determined not to lose the war. When she jerked hard on Bridie's arm, Ruth suddenly lost her balance and tipped backward and ... fell.

Down, down, down she went, into the deep blackness.

"Bridie!" Ruth screamed. *"Bridie!"*

17

Ruth landed hard on her behind, her whole body jarring on impact.

Ouch! That hurt. She shook her head and tried to get her thoughts in order.

She was sitting on the bank next to the big rock, with the curving expanse of brown water only a meter away. Her bum really hurt where she had landed on it, and she had grime and dust all over her clothes. And . . . there was no Bridie.

"Rodney!" she shouted. "Rodney, where are you? I just know you're here somewhere!"

But all was quiet and there was no sign of the rat.

Gradually, as the full extent of Bridie's plight hit Ruth, she became more and more upset. Against all the odds, within just a few hours they'd become such good friends. In fact, Bridie was the nicest person her own age that Ruth had ever met; and more than that, she desperately needed help, and *much more than that,* Ruth owed her! It was Ruth who had enticed Bridie into risking everything with promises of a new life, and then at the very last moment only Ruth had been able to escape, leaving poor Bridie behind! She had ditched her! And Ruth wasn't the only one to blame.

"That creepy little . . . *rat!*" Ruth muttered furiously under her breath. "He *knew* something like this would happen. I just know he did." Her anger toward the rat mixed with her concern for Bridie until fury was rolling through her in giant waves. She'd asked for no family and been hurled back to a virtual jail in the 1950s! How dumb was he? Or perhaps he'd *meant* to freak her out. Whatever the reason, there was no way she could leave Bridie in such a dire situation. No way in the world!

Ruth picked up a few stones and flung them into the river. She must find a way to get back to that place and time. She didn't care if she had to stay there forever. Well, she did care, of course, but . . . she was prepared to do it.

She sat down on the large rock, staring in front of her for a while until the thick, anxious feeling rose up and blocked her throat. This time she couldn't do anything about it. Tears spilled down her cheeks. She wiped them away with both fists, but more arrived to take their place, until her whole face felt like one hot, sore bruise. She knew that she probably looked a fright too, but she didn't care. If only Howard would come back—at least she'd have someone to tell.

What to do? She knew what she *should* do, but without

the rat, what *could* she do? Returning to that school would be impossible without him. She hadn't planned on spending the rest of her life back in the twentieth century, but if that was the only way she could save Bridie, then she'd do it. Her mum and dad had been kids not so long after that time and they'd survived, hadn't they? If both Bridie and she ended up at Barrytown for the rest of their lives, then so be it! They would manage somehow. They almost managed to get away once, so who was to say they wouldn't succeed the next time?

But she couldn't do anything without Rodney. Ruth gave a deep sigh. The sun had come out from behind a cloud and the warmth comforted her a little.

Suddenly, she heard a slight scratching sound. She held her breath and waited to see if she had imagined it. No. There it was again, followed by a couple of polite throat-clearings. Ruth turned around quickly and . . . there he was.

Rodney was leaning up against a nearby rock.

"Well, hello there," he said in an unconcerned tone. "I take it things were not exactly to your liking?"

Ruth stared at him furiously, not trusting herself to even speak.

He looked different this time, fatter and sleeker and more arrogant. A quick, sharp boot in the backside might take that gloating look off his face! And something else was different too.

"I've got glasses," he said, as though able to read her mind, pointing proudly at the wire-rimmed spectacles sitting on the tip of his nose.

Ruth shrugged. As far as she was concerned they looked completely ridiculous, but she didn't bother saying so. She wanted to tell him that rats didn't wear glasses and that he should go get himself a life, but she knew she'd better stay cool and keep him on her side if possible. She needed to give herself the best chance of getting what she wanted.

"I don't know if I told you that I had trouble reading," Rodney prattled on. "When I got these, everything became clearer." He smiled at her, probably able to tell that she was on the point of exploding. "And I can read perfectly now."

Ruth grimaced and turned away. One of Marcus's favorite lines popped into her mind: *Tell someone who cares!*

"Please cut it out, Rodney," Ruth said. "I need to go back there."

The rat frowned, shifted about awkwardly on his two hind feet, and tried to look as though he didn't know what she was talking about.

Ruth peered at him. She could swear that he was faking that *deeply serious* expression. She took a closer look. Yes, there was a smirk hanging around the corners of that mean little mouth. The idea that he was finding the situation funny made her see red.

"Listen, I'm deadly serious," she said. "I've thought it all through. I want to stay there."

The rat walked down to the river and put his toe tentatively in the water and then pulled it out quickly.

"Freezing," he muttered.

"Will you listen to me!" Ruth exploded. "I *demand* to go back."

"But what about your *friend* here?" he said lightly.

"He'll be okay! You promised he would be. It's Bridie I'm worried about!"

With both front paws clasped behind him, the rat began to walk around in circles. After a while he stopped and folded his paws over his bony little chest, and looked away into the distance.

"No can do," he muttered eventually.

"What!" Ruth stood up.

"Absolutely not on."

"Rodney, did you hear me?" Ruth said tersely, taking a few steps toward him. "I *need* to go back there."

He cleared his throat. "That is not really possible, I'm afraid. Sorry about that."

"It has got to be possible! I left a very special person back there who—"

"Look, why don't we sit down and discuss this reasonably?" Rodney said in a firm, kind voice.

"Right," she said through gritted teeth. How dare a sneaky little *rat* patronize her!

Rodney scooted over to the rock that she'd been sitting on and jumped up onto it.

"Do you think we might have something . . . to eat while we talk?" he suggested. "You've got an apple, haven't you?"

Ruth was actually starving, but she decided not to oblige him. She needed to keep him on track and show him just how serious she was.

"We've got business to attend to," she snapped. "When we get that sorted, then we'll eat."

"No point doing business on an empty stomach."

"I'm in a hurry, Rodney." Ruth sat down on a patch of grass.

"Aren't we all?" The rat sighed.

Ruth was finally beginning to understand that Rodney simply didn't have the power to send her back to save Bridie. She lay on her back on the grass and closed her eyes. What a mess! What a complete disaster she had made of everything.

"So, you're telling me it's a total impossibility?"

"No repeats, unfortunately," Rodney said.

Ruth sighed miserably. *What would be happening to Bridie right at that moment?* Sister Gregory's face rose to the surface of her mind. Those mean eyes and the steel grip of her fingers. Ruth lifted her hand to her cheek where the nun had struck her and shivered.

Rodney cleared his throat a couple more times. "You do have one more wish," he said quietly. "I realize that—"

"No way!" Ruth cut him off. "If there's no chance of going back to save Bridie, I'm not even going to think about using that third wish! It can just stay right where it is."

"I think that is a mistake."

"But I've messed up Bridie's life," Ruth wailed. "Totally! If only I could undo that."

"Ah well, I *might* be able to help you there," Rodney said.

"How do you mean?" Ruth sat up quickly.

"I'll have to check," he said thoughtfully, "but I *think* I might just be able to undo what happened from the time you got there. Nothing else, mind . . . just the section of time you were there, but I need to get some independent advice on it."

"Who from?" Ruth asked sharply.

"From my uncle Siggy. He's an expert in this kind of thing. Of course, I would prefer *not* to contact him, but if you're absolutely adamant that you—"

"Ask him!" Ruth commanded loudly. "You must ask him! Please."

Rodney winced. "No point getting flustered."

"I'm not flustered!" Ruth snarled, on the point of tears.

"All right"—Rodney was pointedly polite—"but I've got to find him. I'll be as quick as I can."

"Okay," she agreed. What choice did she have?

Ruth saw that one of her shoelaces had come undone. She bent over to retie it. When she looked up again, the rat was already gone.

She settled herself back on the grass to wait for him, hoping for a change of luck. *Please,* she prayed, *I need to at least undo the harm I've caused!*

While she waited, Ruth watched the sky, and for the first time since she'd arrived at the bridge she felt the stillness around her. There were all kinds of sounds that she hadn't noticed before—nearby twittering birds and the occasional mournful cries of a crow, the rustling of leaves, the bellow of a cow calling her calf. She thought of Howard and wondered how he was getting on with his fishing. If he'd come with her, things might not have been so bad. Then again, a boy wouldn't have much chance in a convent! He might not even have been allowed through the gates.

Ruth noticed that the sun had moved around to the west. Would the rest of her family be back from the bike race yet? Would they be worried about her? Would they miss her if she left forever?

She wished that she were home right at that moment and that none of this had happened. The boys weren't really so bad. Living with a whole bunch of messy, chaotic people might not be the best fun, but it beat a lot of other things. Like having perfect, boring parents breathing down your neck, for example, or being at the mercy of a horrible teacher like Thunder Guts. Or having to feel guilty about causing untold trouble in someone else's life. That one felt particularly bad.

Ruth's eyes grew heavy as she waited for the rat, but there was no way she would give in to it. She owed it to Bridie to stay awake. She must have dozed off, though, because her whole body jerked to attention with Rodney's voice.

"I *can* undo your time there, but . . . there is a catch."

"What?"

"I'm afraid it is contingent on you making use of your last wish."

"Why is that?" Ruth asked suspiciously.

"Just the way it works."

"But I'll only get myself into a heap of new trouble!"

"Up to you." The rat shrugged. "If you don't use it, then things stay as they are for Bridie."

"But why?" Ruth wailed.

"That's just the way this stuff works," he said. "You heading off again works as a kind of circuit breaker, and *that* means I can undo the previous disaster."

"But I don't want to go anywhere else." Ruth moaned. "My family isn't so bad and . . ."

But the rat wasn't interested. He held up one paw for her to be quiet.

"It's up to you," he said sourly. "But it beats me why you wouldn't want to have another go."

"I'll tell you why," Ruth fumed, "because *you* get it so wrong!"

"What was so wrong last time?" the rat muttered.

"When I said a place with discipline and order, I was think-ing of some kind of peaceful retreat somewhere like the Hima-layas or some little community in the hills, *not* a Catholic boarding school in the 1950s!"

"Those places up in the hills are very highly sought after,"

Rodney said defensively. "Places are quite limited. It's the time of the year too. Everyone has the winter blues and they want a quick fix. I told you that I couldn't promise anything too specific. A Catholic boarding school in the fifties was the best I could do."

"That place was a nightmare!" Ruth grumbled.

"And yet you're willing to go back?"

"I want to go back for the friend I made there," Ruth replied hotly.

"Well?" Rodney looked at her askance. *"Hello?"*

"What?"

"Nothing coming together in that head of yours yet?"

"What are you talking about?"

"Are you telling me that you haven't realized?"

"What?"

"Anywhere is good if you've got a friend."

Ruth sniffed and looked away, absolutely *hating* the fact that he was telling her something that might have a grain of truth in it.

"What if you're in jail?" she mumbled sullenly. "A friend isn't going to help there."

"It will make things a lot easier." The rat chuckled. "Last time I was incarcerated I certainly found that the friends I made there—" He stopped. "Never mind."

"Go on, Rodney."

"No."

"Is there something you're not telling me, Rodney?"

"Not at all."

Ruth looked at him severely, but the rat wouldn't meet her eyes. She sighed. There was probably a mountain of information she should know about Rodney, but somehow now wasn't the right time.

"What about if your house is smashed to bits by a cyclone?" she said stiffly. "A friend won't put it back together for you."

"A true friend will stick out the bad times with you," Rodney declared pompously, "and that is an enormous help."

"If your parents both die horribly in a car accident, then—"

"Oh, for goodness' sake!" Rodney snapped. "Could we please at least stick to the case in hand? Are you telling me that everything apart from your friend was bad about that place?"

"Not exactly," Ruth said in a small voice. "Sister Winifred was kind of interesting—a good teacher, anyway. I think I would have gotten to like her if I'd stayed. And I suppose I did like the fact that there wasn't chatter all the time. I liked the silent times. And I liked the singing. I was looking forward to learning the words. I would have liked to join in the singing every morning."

"See!" the rat said triumphantly.

"But some of it was terrible!"

"Welcome to the real world!" Rodney said. Ruth frowned and wondered all over again why she'd been so keen to find him.

"But it's not the real world, is it?"

"Well, no." Rodney gave one of his dry chuckles and they both started laughing at the same time. "Not *exactly* the real world. No."

"Okay." Ruth felt a little easier after the laugh. "I'm willing to have another go if you make things better for Bridie."

"Done!"

"Do you promise?"

"I promise." Rodney was shifting from one foot to the other. "So let's get going quickly, because I'm due back for the races."

"*What?*" Ruth's mouth fell open.

"I've got a lot riding on a little guy called Pick-Me-Up. He's—"

"Is Pick-Me-Up a . . . *rat?*" Ruth was trying to imagine a race meeting of rats. Would they have callers and racetracks and judges and ribbons for the winner?

"Well, of course he's a rat!" Rodney waved the question away irritably. "So annoying, the way humans think they are the only ones who do anything interesting!"

"Okay, okay." Ruth sighed. "Let's keep our minds on the job."

An hour later they were still discussing Ruth's options. It was her last chance; she didn't want to get it wrong.

"You're smart," the rat was saying. "Maybe we could try and get you into the NASA space program."

"I'm only eleven," Ruth reminded him.

"Wouldn't you like to be the first kid in space?"

Ruth thought for a while. "Not that much," she said. "I've always thought it would be kind of boring being up there and having to eat out of tubes and ... how would you go to the toilet?"

"There are plastic bags inside your bodysuit."

"Yuck! And it would be so hard to get back if I hated it."

"True, but not ... impossible."

"Not space," Ruth said decisively. "Thanks all the same."

"Well, what about being part of an exploration team? Deep in the heart of Africa?"

"Now you're talking!" Ruth was delighted. "I wouldn't mind that."

"Going to places that no one has seen before," Rodney said enthusiastically. "There are still places like that on the planet, you know, Ruth."

"Hmmm." Ruth tried to imagine what it would be like. She was excited by the idea until a mental image came to her out of the blue. There she was in the intense heat, trudging along behind a group of adults. She was thirsty, her feet were sore, and they were about to walk through crocodile-infested waters. "Actually, Rodney, I don't think so. I don't like really hot weather, and what about those weird insects that give you exotic diseases? I haven't been inoculated. What if I got really sick? I might die."

"Well, you're going to have to think of something!" the rat snapped. "I told you before, I don't have all day." He flung what was left of his apple core into the river.

Ruth noticed that his stomach was as enormous as a duck egg. He was shifting about trying to get comfortable and she wanted to ask him if all rats were greedy or if it was just him.

"You're going to have to make a decision soon. What would you really like?"

Ruth closed her eyes and tried to think.

"Remember, this isn't only about you."

Ruth opened her eyes. "How do you mean?"

"My career is going off the rails." The rat sniffed.

"Really?"

Rodney gave a deep sigh. "I've simply got to get this one right or I'm . . . custard."

"Okay." Ruth closed her eyes again. The pressure was on now.

"Have you got a secret desire?" he said slyly. "Right at the bottom of your heart?"

Still with her eyes closed, Ruth threw away her core and lay back on the grass. "Well, I suppose I do," she said after a while, beginning to blush furiously. If only it were something more interesting! But there was nothing for it. This was her last chance at the life she'd really like, so she'd better come clean.

"So what is it?" Rodney was looking at her intently.

"I want to *be somebody*." Ruth's face was bright red.

"Somebody?" the rat repeated, frowning.

"I want to stand out from the crowd."

"Oh." Rodney's mouth twitched. "I see. Have you got a field in mind? Where you'd like to excel?"

"Not really," she mumbled.

"Sports?"

"No!" She shook her head. "Definitely not."

"Music?"

"No."

"What about performing, then? Acting, theater, or the circus?"

"No way!" Ruth exclaimed. "Marcus is good at sports and music, and my little brother is a born actor. He'll end up a performer of some sort, for sure. I want my *own* thing that I'm really good at."

"Hmmm." The rat shook his head. "So . . . what *are* you good at?"

"I don't know," Ruth said glumly. "Not much except spelling and liberal arts, math and geography and history." She sighed. "You can't really *be somebody* with any of that, can you?"

"Well, that remains to be seen," the rat muttered. "Just give me a few minutes, will you?"

Ruth watched him walk down toward the river, both paws behind his back, head lowered; he was frowning and obviously thinking hard.

She doubted he'd be able to do anything good with what she wanted, but with a bit of luck it wouldn't be quite as bad as the other two wishes. *Remember*, she told herself sternly, *this is all about getting Bridie out of a very big hole.*

"What sort of family do you want this time?" Rodney called.

"My old one will do," Ruth said.

"Really?" Rodney stared at her in surprise.

Ruth thought of the dead eyes of her mum and dad in the perfect version and nodded.

"What about the laptop and the swimming pool?" the rat asked, genuinely incredulous.

Ruth sighed. "I suppose there's no chance of having the *old* family with the good house, laptop, and swimming pool ... and without the friends?"

She knew she was pushing things, but it might be worth a try.

"I don't do mix and match," the rat said crossly. "Are you sure?"

"Yes! How many times do I have to say it?"

"Okay. So the old family"—the rat shook his head—"in the old house with all the mess and ... and the rest of it?"

"Yes." Ruth sighed.

"Well, well, there is no accounting for—"

"Just shut up, okay?"

"Very well."

"By the way, have you got any paper and a pencil? I want to write Howard a note."

"A note?" Rodney was suspicious.

"I want to tell him to go back on his own if I'm away too long."

Rodney produced a blank page from his trouser pocket and then a pencil from his boot.

Ruth wrote a quick note to Howard and put it under a rock near where he'd been lying asleep. She didn't want him to wait for her and get into more trouble than he needed to with his father.

"I think I might have something," Rodney said after a few moments of silent thought.

"Really?" Ruth was excited, until she remembered how wrong things could get. "Is it possible for you to run through some details with me first?"

"No, it isn't!" Rodney said angrily. "That *isn't* how this works!"

"Okay! Keep your shirt on. I didn't mean to insult you."

"My *work* involves very sophisticated skills."

"I'm sure it does," Ruth muttered apologetically. "I didn't mean to imply . . ."

"Believe me, I want this one to work just as much as you do. You're going to have to trust me."

18

"Crunch time, ladies and gentlemen! Whoever wins this round of *Brain Box* will be Victorian state champion and will go on to compete in the national final next week."

There was a loud rolling drumbeat followed by a bouncy guitar riff.

"Please give our two contestants a hand!"

Enthusiastic clapping and catcalling, along with a few whistles, drowned out the music.

Ruth blinked as her eyes adjusted. There was a sea of strange faces in front of her. She looked around and felt herself go a little woozy.

She was sitting in a kind of booth, and the lights were so bright she could hardly see. A man in a snappy suit with silver hair and his face covered in makeup was standing about a meter away from her; on the other side of him sat a boy roughly her age dressed in a white shirt and tie. The boy's hair was combed up into spikes. Her own long hair had been set into tight curls that fell to her shoulders and were stiff with lacquer. It felt a little like having an animal on her head. What was she doing in front of all these people? *Where on earth was she?*

She looked up. Huge lights were beaming down from the ceiling. A couple of enormous black swivel cameras pointed at the three of them on the stage. She must be in a television studio! Ruth was overcome with an intense desire to get up and run. A shy person wanting to *be somebody*! And that idiot rat thought she meant in the actual spotlight and famous—that wasn't what she'd meant at all. What could she have been thinking to trust him *again*?

"So in case you've just joined us at home"—the man with the silver hair was looking directly into the camera with a wide, oily smile—"we have Leon and Ruth, and they are slogging it out to make it to our final!" He turned to them. "Tell me, are you guys ready?"

"Yes, sir!" Leon said with a confident grin, and the audience clapped wildly.

"And Ruth?"

"Yes . . . sir," Ruth said nervously.

The applause for her was more subdued.

"Okay, this is the big one!" the man said.

The drumbeat rolled again and the audience went quiet.

"First on the buzzer gets the chance to answer."

Ruth looked down at the button in front of her. As though on autopilot, she positioned her hand above it.

"In what year did man first walk on the moon?"

He had to be kidding. *That was way too easy.* But maybe it was a trick question? The boy was frowning, probably trying to work out the same thing. Ruth decided to go with what she knew. If it was a trick question, then she might as well get it over with. She pressed the buzzer and the man invited her to answer.

"1969," she said, then added, "Sir."

"And you are absolutely right!" the man shouted, and the crowd went wild. *"Go, Ruth! Go!"*

In spite of her nerves Ruth felt a buzz of excitement. If the questions were all this easy, she might actually win!

"Spell *accommodation*," was the next question. Of course Ruth knew how to spell that, but the boy beat her to the buzzer. Annoyed with herself for being slow, Ruth decided to really concentrate. The drumbeat started rolling again. This must be it. She tensed up in anticipation. *She wouldn't let him beat her again!*

"Who was the first Queen Elizabeth's father?" the man asked.

There was a hushed silence, but not for long. Ruth pushed her buzzer, just beating Leon.

"Henry VIII," she said matter-of-factly.

"And Ruth is absolutely correct. Henry VIII was Queen Elizabeth's father. Ladies and gentlemen, we have a winner! Will you all please go ballistic for Ruth Craze!"

The applause began and built quickly to a crescendo. It flooded Ruth's ears and swirled around her head like a barrage of thunderclaps.

The man came over, took her hand, and pulled her up out of her seat. "The winner, ladies and gentlemen: Ruth Craze! Take a bow, Ruth!"

Ruth stood holding hands with the man in front of the huge crowd, thinking that just maybe Rodney had gotten it right.

"Here is your check for ... ten thousand dollars!"

More drums, and two pretty blond women brought out an enormous signed check.

Ten thousand dollars! To think it was now actually hers! *She was ... a winner.*

"And that's our show, ladies and gentlemen! Don't forget to tune in next week, when Ruth will be competing against all the other state finalists ... when we'll find out who the national *Brain Box* champion is! Good luck, Ruth!" the man yelled. "We're all behind you."

"Good luck, Ruth!" the crowd echoed as the show closed. "Good luck!"

The lights went down and the cameras backed away and everyone relaxed. About to step off the stage, Ruth was intercepted by hugs and whoops of congratulation from members of the crew.

"Fantastic, girl!"

"Good for you, Ruth!"

Ruth noticed that her opponent was sitting in his booth all alone, looking very disappointed. She pushed through the throng of people surrounding her and walked over to him.

"Thanks, Leon," she said awkwardly, not knowing what else to say, only that she wanted to make him feel better.

"Congratulations," he said, holding out his hand, "you did real good, Ruth."

"But so did you," Ruth said quickly. "That last one was a bit of a fluke for me." This was actually a small lie; she loved reading about the kings and queens of England. "It was just luck, you know."

"Tell that to my parents," he said, pointing to a couple standing near the door away from everyone else. A big sour-looking man was dressed in a fawn business suit. Next to him stood a very heavily made-up woman dressed in a white linen suit with lots of gold jewelry around her wrists and neck. They both looked very glum.

"They're going to be so mad." Leon sighed.

"What will they say?"

"They'll say I didn't put enough work in."

"But that's crazy," Ruth protested. "I mean, you were within one point of winning!"

"I know. . ." He shrugged unhappily. "But my brother wins everything."

Ruth took another look at the couple. She would have liked

to go up and tell them that it was terrible to expect so much of their kid, but of course she didn't.

"They your parents?" Leon asked as he stood up. She looked over to where her mum and dad, Marcus, and Paul were sitting in the front row smiling proudly.

"Yeah," she murmured. Her mum was waving now, in full view of everyone. Ruth gave a small wave and then turned away. Her mother had on a bright pink knitted dress that didn't really suit her figure at all.

"They look nice."

"Thanks," Ruth said humbly. Well, at least they'd never give her a hard time for not winning something like this. She shook Leon's hand again and was about to run down the stairs to greet her family when the silver-haired game show host stopped her. He wasn't quite so enthusiastic or friendly now that the lights were down.

"See you next week," he said. "Make sure you get here a good hour before we're due on."

"Okay," Ruth said. "What happens now?"

"Cindy will look after you," he said with a tight smile.

By the time Ruth got to her parents and brothers they were surrounded by a group of people who were slapping them on the back and congratulating *them*.

"Amazing girl you have there," someone was saying warmly.

"You must all be so proud."

"Well, yes, we are," her father's voice boomed. "Ruth's always been a bit of a standout. She could read at four."

Ruth pushed through the crowd and elbowed him in the ribs.

But her father was on a roll. "Of course, she was in the accelerated program at school."

"Dad!"

"Oh, here she is!" Her mother turned around and opened her arms. "Good for you, Ruthie!"

"Thanks, Mum."

"How did you know that last one, Ruth?" Marcus asked quietly, his voice full of awe. "I wouldn't have had a clue about Queen Elizabeth's father."

"If you win next week, you get a trip for two to America!" Paul said excitedly. "Have you thought about who you're going to ask?" He was looking at her with such longing that it made everyone laugh.

"I probably won't win," Ruth said.

"Of course you'll win." Her mother was smiling proudly. "I just know it."

Try as she might, Ruth couldn't help feeling a glow of pleasure when she saw that her whole family was so proud.

"Bye, Ruth," Leon called as he made his way out of the studio between his disgruntled parents. "Good luck for next week."

"Thanks, Leon."

"Excuse me, Ruth." A glamorous-looking, orange-haired woman in her twenties, dressed in a tight red suit and extremely high heels, interrupted them. "I'm Cindy from the network, and I'll be looking after you for the rest of the week."

"Oh, hello," Ruth said shyly. The woman was so perfectly made up that she looked like a doll. "This is my mum and dad and my brothers."

Cindy nodded curtly and handed Mr. Craze a printout without really looking at him. "Here's a copy of Ruth's itinerary for the rest of the day. As you will see, we've booked her into the Hilton Hotel for three nights, assuming that's okay with you?"

"The Hilton!" Mr. and Mrs. Craze chorused.

"Well, it's much easier to get to places from there because you're, like, way out in . . ." She frowned and looked down at her notebook. "I'm sorry, I don't even know where that is."

"Well . . ."

"I guess . . ."

"You'll have a big, beautiful room all to yourself," Cindy said, smiling down at Ruth, "your own bathroom, and whenever you want anything, you just have to ring down for room service. Night or day."

Ruth nodded, trying to imagine what that might mean. "So, if I want a milkshake in the middle of the night . . . ?" She looked at her brothers, who were almost choking with envy.

"Or a hot pie and a Coke." Cindy laughed. "Or your clothes

ironed or access to the Internet . . . all you do is just pick up the phone." Ruth stared at her, openmouthed. "Think you can handle *that*?"

"I'm afraid we don't have the money for that sort of thing," Mrs. Craze said awkwardly.

"You don't pay a cent!" Cindy gave her a condescending smile. "The show will be picking up the tab, and please don't worry about her. I'll be in the room right next door. Each morning I'll take Ruth to whatever media events are happening that day. Staying in a hotel will be a great experience for her," Cindy said, reaching out and squeezing Ruth's arm, "and it will make the whole week leading up to the final much easier to manage."

"I think she might be a bit young," Mrs. Craze said. "To stay in a hotel room on her own, I mean," she added. They all looked at Ruth, who was trying not to look as nervous as she felt. But she'd been thinking the same thing.

"What do *you* say, Ruth?" Cindy asked.

"I'll be fine," Ruth said quickly. She'd never been inside a fancy hotel before. Not even on the ground floor. Imagine being a guest there!

"I'll be fine," she said again, more firmly.

"Good girl!" Cindy turned to Mr. and Mrs. Craze. "Think of it as a great . . . opportunity." She consulted her notebook again. "Now, that's about all, I think," she said, putting a hand on Ruth's arm. "Want to come and have a look at those prizes?"

"But I've got my prize," Ruth said, holding up the check.

"Oh, I've got loads more for you!" Cindy gave her a toothy smile and winked. "I think you'll be pleased." She looked at the rest of the family. "There's no need for you to hang around. I'll take care of her," she said.

Ruth saw the disappointment on all their faces and felt bad—for her brothers, especially. At the same time, she couldn't help seeing them all through Cindy's perfectly made-up eyes. Her parents looked so wretchedly old-fashioned and so badly matched. Never before had she noticed just how skinny and tall her father was compared with her short, dumpy mother.

"Ruth?" Marcus was actually begging her with his eyes.

Ruth turned to look at Cindy, who reluctantly relented. "Well, you could come by for a few minutes to take some of the prizes home," she said. "I assume you drove here?"

Mr. Craze nodded.

"Off we go, then."

Cindy linked arms with Ruth and led the way back into the building through a long windowless corridor, and the rest of the family followed. Ruth glanced behind at them occasionally. The boys were excited, but her parents seemed uneasy. She'd be glad when they did go home and she could get on with dealing with . . . whatever was going to happen next.

As they followed Cindy's clicking stilettos down the corridor, every now and then a door would open and a famous face would peep out.

"Hi, Ruth!" said the guy who read the news. "Well done! I know you'll kill 'em next week."

"Thanks . . . Mr. . . ."

"It's Kevin." He grinned.

"Thanks, Kevin."

"Good for you, Ruth," a pretty blond woman said, beaming. "My whole family was rooting for you. So cool under pressure! You really should consider a career in the media."

"Thanks." It wasn't until she got a little closer that Ruth saw that the woman was from *The Breakfast Show*, and behind her, getting his makeup fixed, was her sidekick—the two most popular television personalities in the country. The man got up from his chair and came to the door.

"What a clever girl you are!" he said, and then smiled at the rest of the family. "You guys must be thrilled."

"Oh, we are!" her mum said shyly.

"Very proud," her father mumbled.

Ruth could see that they were both a bit overwhelmed. They loved *The Breakfast Show*.

"We'll be watching next week!"

"Thank you."

Ruth and her family followed Cindy around a corner and then headed down another corridor.

"*Hello, Ruth!*" came a loud, vaguely familiar voice behind them. "Or should I be saying *G'day, Einstein?*" The Crazes all turned to see Frankie Lee—complete with tatts and dreadlocks, fancy silver jewelry and black leather jacket—beaming at Ruth. "Wish I had your brains!" he added, sauntering up casually. Marcus stared in awe. Everybody knew that Frankie Lee was the coolest man to grace the small screen ever. He interviewed all the best bands and musicians from around the world, and here he was talking to Marcus's little sister!

"G'day, guys!" Frankie grinned at her brothers and parents but sidled up playfully alongside Ruth. "Hey, Cindy," he said, pulling a tiny silver camera from out of his leather jacket, "can you take a picture of me and Ruth?"

"Sure!" Cindy took the camera. "Up against the wall, you two!"

The rest of the family edged away as Frankie put his arm around Ruth. Cindy flirted outrageously as she arranged the shot, giggling at Frankie's jokes. Ruth stood smiling stiffly into the camera, aware of her family's awed expressions. *Could this really be happening?*

"Thanks," said Frankie as he took the camera from Cindy. "Someday that one will be worth a million!" He waved good-bye and disappeared back into his dressing room. Ruth caught the look of stunned envy on her brothers' faces and a spurt of wicked pleasure bubbled up inside her.

Cindy led them into a large windowless room. There were a couple of overstuffed sofas and chairs and a big round table. But over in the corner was another table piled high with boxes of all shapes and sizes.

"All that is for you," Cindy said with a smile, pointing at the boxes. "Do you want to have a look now?"

"What is it?" Ruth smiled back uncertainly.

"Everything you can think of!" Cindy said. "Every company in the country wanted to be part of the show. These are the prizes they donated for the finalist."

"But what have I won?"

"Well, let's have a look, shall we?"

Her parents stared blankly as cameras, watches, iPods, computers, and even a plasma television were pulled from box after box. Ruth's attention was caught by a small package next to the fancy television. Within moments she had unwrapped the coolest little mobile phone. It was silver gray with a stripe of black dots down each side. Except for Marcus, who had a crappy old thing whose battery was always running out, no one in the family even had a mobile phone! This one was so slim and sharp-looking . . . And you could take photos with it and send e-mails and watch telly.

"Can I keep this?"

"Sweetheart, you get to keep everything!" Cindy waved at

the table. "It's all yours, and there'll be more—much more—next week if you win."

"Does she get to keep *all* of this?" Mrs. Craze asked doubtfully.

"Of course she does," Cindy said. "She's the state champion!"

"But I'm not sure we've got room in our house," Mr. Craze protested.

"Maybe it's time to put on an extension, then," Cindy retorted. She looked at her watch and frowned. "I'm afraid we've really got to get moving." She gave Ruth a fresh version of her toothy smile. "There's a live interview at ten and heaps of press after that. This is our highest-rating show at the moment, so management wants maximum media coverage over the next week, in the lead-up to the national finals, but . . . are you hungry, Ruth?"

Ruth nodded. She was starving.

"What time is it?" she asked.

"Nine o'clock," Cindy replied. "What do you say to breakfast?"

Ruth's brothers' eyes lit up at the mention of food. Mr. and Mrs. Craze looked hopeful too. Everyone was waiting to see what Ruth would say. She felt dizzy with her newly acquired power.

"Great," she said. "Can my family come too?"

"I actually don't think it's a good idea, if you don't mind," Cindy said, looking at Mr. and Mrs. Craze. The boys' faces fell. "But perhaps you'll take care of all this?" She pointed at the boxes.

"Yes, of course," Mr. Craze said. "Come on, boys." Ruth and

Cindy watched as the boxes were piled up and shared out among her family to carry.

"All right, then," Cindy said briskly. "You'll be able to find your way out?"

"I . . . think so."

"Just follow the exit signs. Oh, and we'll be in touch about this afternoon."

"Will you be all right, Ruthie?" Mrs. Craze asked.

"Of course," Ruth said.

"Don't worry, we won't touch any of it, Ruth," her father said. "We'll put it all in your room for you to have when you get back, won't we, boys?"

They nodded miserably.

"Okay, thanks." Ruth watched them all troop out of the room carrying her stuff, wishing she didn't feel so . . . like she'd let them down in some way. "I don't mind if you look at everything," she called after them.

The dining room was very plush, with creamy white walls and carpet that was thick and soft to walk on. Half a dozen nicely set polished wood tables were placed around the room, some already occupied by glamorous people, all eating and talking and laughing. Most of them stopped as Cindy walked in with Ruth, and light clapping broke out.

"Well done, Ruth!" someone called.

"Here's the Quiz Kid Wonder!"

"Just the beginning, kid," called the man from *Media Today*. "You're on your way!"

"Thanks!" Ruth now had an inkling of what royalty must feel like when they walked into a room and everyone knew who they were.

Cindy led her to one of two tables in the nicest part of the room, right near a big window overlooking the river. While Cindy was calling the waiter over to take their order, Ruth took a few moments to look out the window and marvel at the river twisting and turning like a glistening brown snake below. She had never seen the city from this high up. If she did go on to have a career in television, she'd be able to work in a place like this every day.

"I need to run through our schedule for the day," said Cindy when the food arrived. "Just go on with your breakfast and I'll tell you about it."

"Okay." Ruth picked up her knife and fork and attacked her eggs on toast. For some reason she wasn't quite as hungry as she'd been before. It was probably just nerves.

"First up, there's the live interview with Gordon Blake. You know the show?"

"Not really."

"Just a chat show. He'll introduce you as the state finalist. Then he'll ask you how it feels to be a winner and what your hopes are for the future." She laughed a little. "You feel comfortable doing that?"

"I guess so," Ruth said nervously.

"Then we have a couple of other interviews. *The Sun* is going to do a feature article about you and Bindi Irwin. Subject is 'Amazing Aussie Kids.' You okay with that?" Cindy was speaking so fast that Ruth could barely keep up. "All will want to do their own photos, so we'll take you down to wardrobe first up. Okay so far?"

Ruth nodded, wondering what would happen if she said no.

"And later on in the afternoon a crew will go around to your house and we'll film an 'At Home with Ruth Craze' segment for Wednesday's *Home* show."

What? Ruth put her knife and fork down. "But that show is about *houses!*" she said.

"Not exactly," Cindy replied. "Melissa will interview you at your home, maybe on a sofa or in your kitchen. Then we'll move from room to room, and you can tell us all about your house. Memories, special objects, who does the cooking, et cetera."

"I don't think so," Ruth said, appalled.

"Really?" Cindy looked startled. "Why not?"

"It's just that our house is . . . not very nice."

"Oh, don't worry about that!" Cindy gave a fluttery little wave. "It'll be fine. They'll do some quick interviews with your parents and brothers. It will be over before you know it and we'll have a little showcase of Ruth Craze's life."

"Our house," Ruth stammered, "is a sort of . . ." She was unable to say the word *dump*, but that was what she meant. Their house was a complete dump! No way could it be filmed for a home show!

"Doesn't matter," Cindy said firmly. "Family homes are fine every once in a while."

But Ruth was picturing the family bathroom. The yellow, stained basin and smelly toilet, the pile of damp towels in the corner, the broken tiles and patches of mold growing in the shower recess and the taped-over broken window. "I told your parents that we'd film only what you guys are comfortable with," Cindy said hurriedly when she noticed Ruth's expression. "Honestly."

"So Mum and Dad know about this?"

"Sure," Cindy said. "They're fine."

But what about the dog hair all over the sofa? Ruth wanted to say. *And the grease-laden stove that hasn't been cleaned since Marcus thought he'd make hamburgers for his cycling team two weeks ago?* It was bad enough actually *living* in their house without letting everyone else see it. Nothing about their house belonged on television... *except as a joke!* What could her mother have been thinking to agree to it?

The next few hours zipped by in a haze of frenzied activity. First she went to the wardrobe department and a stylist came up with a whole lot of new ideas about how she should look, along with about a dozen complete sets of new clothes. After the live interview someone took off her heavy television makeup and then redid it more subtly for the photo shoot. Someone else came by to muck around with her hair. She got a new style for each different photographer and lots of pleasant chitchat from everyone.

"God, you are such a star, Ruth!" The makeup guy sighed. "How did you get to be so clever?"

"You've got fabulous hair, Ruth!" the hairdresser said. "Mind if we trim the front a bit?"

Ruth had never had this much attention in her whole life. It felt weird at first, all of them hovering around asking her if she was comfy and would she mind sitting here or there and would she mind putting on a hat for the photo and then could she take it off again *please*. But after a couple of hours she got quite used to it; in fact, it didn't take long before she accepted it as normal, more or less. Yes, she was happy to wear those red boots, but not the brown ones. She'd always hated brown. "Sure, honey! Whatever! Bring over the red boots in her size, will you, Dean?"

"What happens to all the clothes at the end of this?" Ruth asked, fingering a light gray wool sweater longingly.

"You have them, of course, Ruthie." Carol the props girl was busy showing her how to thread the belt through a pair of new five-hundred-dollar jeans. "It's part of the deal."

The reporters were all nice too, and they asked the same questions, so after the first interview there was nothing even vaguely scary or intimidating about talking to them.

"Do you go to bed early, Ruth?"

"How many hours of studying do you do every day?"

"What do your friends think of your success?"

"What is your favorite meal?"

• • •

Before heading back to the hotel to settle in, Ruth had lunch in the dining room. She was sitting with the crew, tucking into spicy sausage rolls and steak fries and an Italian soft drink, when the realization came to her in a flash. *Being a star was totally great!* Apart from a few little downers like having to stand in one position for the photographers and having to smile when you didn't feel like it, she couldn't think of a nicer lifestyle. *Yes,* she thought as she picked another sweet pastry off the little glass plate that had been brought in especially for her. *At last he got it right! Thank you, Rodney!*

But by the time Ruth got back to the hotel and walked into the plush lobby, she was totally exhausted.

Cindy took her by the arm and led her to the elevator. "You look like you could do with a rest," she said. "We've got an hour-long window in our schedule. What about chilling out in front of the telly? Or you can have a swim in the heated pool or … ring your friends."

"Okay." Ruth stumbled into the elevator ahead of Cindy, and within only a matter of seconds they were on the fifteenth floor. Cindy opened the door for her and ushered her into a beautiful room overlooking the park and, past that, the city. Such a big room and all to herself! The furniture—a desk, chair, and enormous bed—was made of polished wood with deep green leather trimmings. Ruth stood and stared around in wonder.

"So you think you'll be okay here, Ruth?"

Ruth looked over at Cindy, who was busily setting some biscuits and a bottle of soft drink on the coffee table.

"Oh, sure. I'll be fine. Thanks, Cindy."

Cindy was looking at her watch. "How about I show you a few things and then leave you alone for a while?"

"Sure," Ruth said. She was actually longing for Cindy to leave so she could examine everything in the room properly.

Cindy showed her the room service menu and the phone and how to ring reception. Then she showed her the bathroom and how the shower worked. The luxury almost shocked Ruth. There were gold faucets and a big fluffy white towel, little packets and bottles of shampoo, and the bathtub was huge.

There was a knock on the door, and a man brought in a small case.

"We sent someone out to buy a few things for you," Cindy said. "Toothbrush and pajamas and other bits and pieces."

"Wow!" Ruth was overwhelmed. "Thank you so much."

"So have a little rest, okay?" Cindy said, showing her again how the taps worked. "Now, don't hesitate to call me if—"

"I'll be fine," Ruth reassured her again.

"We'll get back from your house around four," Cindy said, "have another rest period, and then I'll pick you up for dinner. You'll be free at eight. You can come back here and watch telly;

then up bright and early tomorrow. Okay? Remember, if you want anything, I'm in 108. Only a few doors down on the right."

"Thanks, Cindy."

First off, Ruth examined the contents of the little case. Just as Cindy had said, there were all the essentials, like pajamas and a toothbrush and toothpaste, plus a couple of interesting books and magazines. She wandered around the room, touching the polished wood of the desk and the marble bath and the gold taps, and imagined herself as a grown-up woman, like Cindy, expensively dressed and checking into rooms like this all over the world. Would she ever get used to it? Maybe it would seem quite normal after a while.

She sighed and flopped down on the big bed, then picked up and opened a magazine, wishing that the big room didn't feel so empty somehow. If only she had insisted that Marcus and Paul come back with her. They would both enjoy it all so much—the huge sparkling bathroom, the view over the city, the enormous television screen. She could almost see them. Paul would be buzzing around pointing out one thing after another. *Cool!* He'd be pressing buttons and opening cupboards and checking out everything. *You seen this?* Marcus would lie back on the bed with his hands behind his head and laugh. "It's a hard life," he'd mutter, "but someone's got to live it. Might as well be me!"

20

Ruth got into the big black company car accompanied by Cindy and Melissa the interviewer, Greg the cameraman, and Greg's assistant, Ian. There was a lot of chatter and joking among them about other people working at the network, none of whom Ruth knew. But every now and again they'd say something to include her, so she never felt completely out of it. She was nervous about having these people in her house but realized that there was nothing she could do except take Cindy at her word. What harm would a quick interview with her parents do? Maybe it would all be in close-ups, and no one need see anything of the house.

Only a few minutes into their drive they passed St. Paul's Cathedral and stopped at a red light. Looking out the window, Ruth got a jolt when she noticed a distinctive red door set into the stonework on a small laneway at the back of the cathedral. She stared at it in shock. How would she find her way back there if . . . she needed to?

"Can you tell me the name of that little lane we just passed?" she asked the driver.

"Chapman," he said.

"So many laneways in the city," Cindy murmured. "I haven't been down most of them myself."

Their car pushed on through the traffic. Ruth tried to memorize some landmarks, but after the driver took a few turns, she had to give up. All the buildings started to merge into one another and she had no idea where she was. She tried not to worry. After such a fantastic morning, she couldn't imagine wanting to go back to her former life anyway. Experience may have taught her that things can change, and often very quickly, but she had a strong feeling that this time Rodney really had done it.

As they turned the corner and pulled onto Wales Street, it was as though she were seeing the street for the first time, and the effect was devastating. Not a tree in sight and rubbish everywhere and their house: *the worst house in the street by far!* It looked like it was sinking into the ground. The whole roofline was uneven. Ruth had never noticed that before. Why didn't her father fix up those veranda posts the way he had said he would? This was going to be so humiliating. What were these people going to think? The whole day had been spent sitting and standing and walking on spotless, gleaming surfaces with perfectly groomed, polite people who had probably never seen a dirty fridge or heard someone fart or burp or yell loudly.

Everyone in the car went quiet as they pulled up outside Ruth's place and got out. Even Cindy had nothing to say. With lowered eyes Ruth led the way through the front gate. Suddenly, the battered front door opened and a smiling Mrs. Craze came hurrying out to greet them, making Ruth cringe with shame. Her mother had on the bizarre red caftan that she'd worn to the Christmas concert and she had a bright red fake flower stuck on the side of her head next to her ear.

"Welcome!" she said too loudly, as though the television crew were her best friends. "We're all ready for you. I even made scones!"

"Oh, that's very nice of you!" said Greg the cameraman as he looked around at the dried-out lawn with skid marks all over it, then at the pile of tires in the corner of the yard and the newspapers all over the porch.

"Now, we did what we could," Mrs. Craze said, following his gaze nervously, "but I'm afraid things are still a little rough around here. We're planning a big renovation next year, aren't we, Ruthie?"

Ruth nodded in humiliation.

"But please come in, everyone." Mrs. Craze held the kicked-in screen door open and they all trooped through into the house.

"Why wait for next year?" Ruth heard Ian mutter under his breath to Greg, who chuckled in appreciation.

"Maybe they're hoping it will fall down first!"

Just inside the front door, Greg turned to Mrs. Craze. "Could we have a look around," he asked, "and check out the best place to do the interview?"

"Oh yes, of course." Mrs. Craze waved them on down the hallway. "Make yourselves at home. But I do think the front room would be best."

When they were out of earshot, Ruth turned on her mother. "You must have been out of your mind! Why did you say they could do this?"

"They said it was important," her mother said quietly, "and that you were willing, so I . . . I didn't want to be a fly in the ointment."

"What?"

"We did what we could, Ruthie," Mrs. Craze added feebly.

"Well, it wasn't enough!" Ruth hissed furiously.

They did the interviewing in the front room, as planned, because it was really the only halfway respectable place.

"What is it like being the only girl in the family, Ruth?"

"What would you like to be when you grow up?"

"What do you think about global warming, Ruth?"

Ruth answered as best she could, but this time found it no fun at all. *Half a day and I've become used to the gleaming surfaces too,* she thought. *Get me out of this dump!* Anyway, what could she say about global warming? She was eleven years old! She was too busy thinking about whether someone might by chance have cleaned the toilet or shifted the pile of newspapers from the corner in the kitchen.

When the interview was over, Ruth looked around the room. Why had she ever thought this room was nice? It wasn't at all. Mary Ellen's piano and table were the only two items of furniture that were even vaguely okay. She'd been interviewed sitting on a grubby, worn sofa that looked like it had come straight out of a Goodwill bin. The windows were streaked with dirt and the curtain was torn. The curtain rod was held together with black electrical tape. Memories of Paul doing chin-ups on it crowded into her head like unwanted guests.

"So, Ruth, you going to show us around?" Greg asked. He had the camera on his shoulder now. "Can we film your room . . . the desk and bookcase where you study?"

"No." Ruth shook her head. "I don't want to do that." She didn't want to admit that there was nothing in her room even resembling a desk or a bookcase. Nor did she have a proper closet. All her clothes were in piles on the floor.

"Okay," Cindy said, "we'll finish up, then." She smiled at Ruth. "Mind if we just get a few establishing shots outside?"

"Okay," Ruth said in a small voice. *What was an establishing shot?*

Ruth had to go to the toilet, and when she came back out she saw that the crew was filming the bathroom next door.

She sidled up to Greg as he was shooting the stained bathtub. He started a little when he saw her.

"Your mum said it's okay, honey," he said in a bright, jovial tone. "Don't worry, we won't use most of it."

So why are you filming it? Ruth wanted to say but didn't dare. She ran back into the kitchen, where her mother was pulling scones from the oven.

"Mum, why did you say they could film everything?" she whispered angrily.

"Well, they seemed to think it was important," Mrs. Craze said, looking a little worried. "I'll be glad when this is over, Ruthie."

"You shouldn't have said it was okay," Ruth said. "I definitely don't want my bedroom filmed!"

"I think they already have it, love," her mother said guiltily.

"If only we'd gotten you that new bedroom suite. Remember last year we were planning to and—"

"Too late," Ruth snapped.

"I'm sure everything will be okay," Mrs. Craze said, trying to be more positive.

"That's what you always say and it hardly ever is!"

"Well, sometimes it is," her mother said, and popped a little bit of scone into her mouth. "I think you'll find that these are okay."

Ruth gave a huge sigh and walked out of the room.

But by the end of an hour they had filmed her parents sitting on the veranda eating scones, along with Marcus sitting on his bike sucking a Slurpee—he saw the camera crew's presence as a chance to promote himself as a champion racer. Paul did his interview sitting on his bed while he played the recorder. Cindy and the crew told her it would make for more interesting television to show the whole house and Ruth decided there was nothing she could do. What did she know? They were the professionals. They probably knew what they were doing.

21

Ruth couldn't move. There was something heavy on her chest. She gasped for breath. *What was happening to her?* Her heart was racing. Where was she?

Gradually, she woke up to find . . . nothing. She was lying on top of the hotel bed, but no one was there. The weight was off her chest, and she could breathe easily again. *A bad dream,* she told herself, *just a bad dream.* She looked over to the window and took some deep breaths. Everything was . . . okay. *Wasn't it?*

The light was failing outside and the room was now full of shadows. How long had she been asleep? She sat up and looked at the clock. It was five thirty now. She still had about fifteen minutes before Cindy was going to pick her up for dinner, and suddenly Ruth didn't want to stay in the room any longer. Why not get out for a few minutes and do something . . . *normal?* Maybe she could go and check out the pool.

Making sure she had her key, Ruth went to the door and pulled it open. Out in the corridor she looked around for some kind of sign that would point her in the right direction. Apart from the *clunk* of the cleaner stacking things on a steel trolley down at the other end, all was hushed quietness. Maybe if she walked to the end of the corridor, she'd see a sign that told her where the pool was. *Ah! Voices.* She would ask someone. Ruth took a few tentative steps toward the noise just as Cindy's laugh rose above the rest of the chatter.

"Can't you see the headline if she wins?" Cindy was giggling wildly. "'Slum Girl Fights Her Way to the Top'!" There was music and the clinking of glasses in the background.

"What about that shed full of useless crap!"

"Talk about eccentrics! That father was a nutcase!"

"And the mother!"

"What about the scones?"

"Like rocks!"

"Did you get a shot of her pulling them out of the oven?"

"Yep."

This was followed by a roar of laughter.

"For God's sake, she looked like a medieval soothsayer in that getup."

"So what else did you get?"

"Everything."

"Our audience is going to lap it up!" Cindy said with a laugh. "Mr. and Mrs. Average in Altona will feel like their own lives are normal and successful in comparison."

"It will work for the show too," Ian said more seriously. "When they see the family the kid comes from, they'll want to see her win."

"Did they all sign the form?"

"You betcha!" Cindy said gaily. "And not a murmur out of any of them."

"So we're safe?"

"Absolutely."

Ruth ran back to her room, her face blazing with humiliation. The "At Home with Ruth Craze" segment would make her family the laughingstock of the country. She shuddered. The flea-ridden dog, her dad's shed of mad inventions, her fat mum's terrible dress sense—they'd caught it all on film! She looked around the room wildly. A wobbly feeling in her chest and tummy made her feel like she might be going to faint. But ... she was on this roller coaster now and there was only one way to stop it. She'd signed those bits of paper and, more importantly, her parents had signed other bits. The whole thing was going to happen!

Suddenly, the phone rang. Ruth jumped and stood staring at it. *Once, twice, three times* ... Ruth tentatively picked it up.

"Yes?" she said.

"Hello." It was her mother's voice. "Ruthie?"

"Mum." The creeping tightness in her throat made it impossible to say much else.

All of a sudden, she wished she were home and that none of this had happened. *Home.* She was actually longing for the familiar smell of it. She would like to be in her own little shoe box of a room watching the night sky outside, hearing those annoying, loud brothers prattling on in the next room.

"Just ringing to make sure you're okay."

A rush of tears flooded Ruth's eyes.

"I'm okay," she said stiffly, feeling like she was choking. "Why wouldn't I be?"

"You don't sound okay," her mother said.

"Mum . . . I just—" She stopped and tried again. "They're going to . . ."

But just at that moment there was a sharp little knock at the door. Ruth let the phone fall and watched it bounce on the carpet. She could hear her mother's voice calling through the phone. *Ruth! You still there?* Ruth's mouth went dry. It would be Cindy; what would she say? There was another knock, and with a sinking heart Ruth said good-bye to her mother and went to the door.

"Ruth, it's time for dinner!" Cindy grinned at her brightly. Ruth thought of how, just moments before, this same woman had been laughing about ruining her entire family. Ruth's heart began to beat hard. She couldn't think of what to say; she just knew she had to get away from her!

"I just . . . need some fresh air for a moment . . .," she mumbled as she ran past Cindy to the elevator and stood there pressing the button frantically until it came.

"Ruth, honey!" Cindy called sharply. The elevator door opened, and Ruth stepped in and pressed the button.

"Don't call me honey," Ruth whispered under her breath.

"Ruth!"

But the door slid shut and Ruth didn't hear any more.

The elevator hit the ground floor with a soft thud. Ruth rushed through the big plush lobby where people were sitting around in fancy clothes chatting over drinks, and almost threw herself at the glass doors leading out into the street. They slid open silently and at last she was outside. The cold air greeted her like a sharp smack in the face. *That felt better.* She stood at the top of the steps, breathing it in greedily. People were coming and going in groups and couples.

By this time next week they'd all know about where she lived. Ruth swallowed hard. All those stupid things she'd said in the interview! If only she could take it all back. The moldy bathroom, the decrepit dog, her father's bizarre shed, and her mother's terrible scones!

Oblivious to the noise, the crowds of people, the cars and trams, and with no clear idea where she was, Ruth walked quickly through the streets. When she turned a corner, she could see the city skyline not far away, so she headed in that direction. Soon she was hurrying down the street with dinner-goers and film patrons, and families on their way to walk along the river. She flew in and out around people, then across roads onto the pavements, past billboards, shops, cafés, and churches, acting like she knew exactly where she was going . . . when she didn't at all.

She was waiting for everything to become clear.

When she came to a big wide bridge, she slowed down and looked back at the tall lit-up city buildings and down at the web of pretty lights along the river. The lovely church just over the bridge, with its high pointy spire reaching right up into the pink-and-gray clouds, looked awesome. No one seemed to be noticing her much now. She stopped, leaning on the side of the bridge for a rest. The new watch, along with all her television clothes, was back in the hotel room, so Ruth had no idea of the time until she saw the town hall clock.

Five minutes to six! Her old life was almost finished.

She walked over to the church and sat down on the steps. When she looked up, to her complete astonishment, she saw her own face on an enormous electronic billboard opposite. The words *Will She Win?* were scrolling under the image, along with news items about sports stars, the economy, and celebrities—all of them underneath her face!

So this was it! Her new life. The show would go to air. Her family would be humiliated and Ruth would become a star.

This is what she'd wished for.

Except it wasn't. Not really.

In one sudden blast, Ruth realized that she didn't want it at all. She wanted a lot, but not this. In spite of . . . everything, she really missed her family. Impractical, loud, messy—what did it matter? She didn't want to see them hurt or humiliated. She loved them!

Ruth stood and ran down the steps and around the side of the building in a complete panic. What could she do? She remembered seeing a red door around these parts earlier that day but couldn't think where. She turned the corner and . . . stopped, hardly able to believe it. Right in front of her was an enormous door with a brass knocker and black steps leading up, and it was bright red!

It was amazing how much slid by in two seconds. She saw herself on television, winning the national championship. She saw herself with all her fantastic new clothes, and all that wonderful stuff, her face on billboards around the city.

It had been so exciting. And fun. Everyone would think she was crazy. But she had to go with her heart.

The red door swung open immediately, and a swish of warm, dank air washed over her face. Ruth threw herself through the opening and plunged down into that dark space.

22

Ruth fell through a cloud of gritty air for what seemed like ages, but was probably only a minute, before landing heavily on the riverbank—this time on her back. Shaky and uncertain, she sat up and slowly looked around.

The pale sunshine had been replaced by long shadows, which meant it was late afternoon or early evening, and gray clouds were piled up along the horizon. Ruth smiled. She'd made it back in one piece.

She got up quickly, shook herself down a bit, then sat on a nearby rock. Her skin was itchy inside her clothes, and there was grime and cobwebs all over her coat, but she was filled with relief. What a day! So much had happened.

Ruth looked over at the place where Howard had lain down to sleep. The note she'd left under the rock was gone. She walked to the bridge and stood resting her elbows on the railing and looking down into the water. What if he was still fishing nearby?

"Howard!" she called loudly. "Hey, Howard! You ready to go?"

She stood still, listening for a reply, and when there was none called again.

"Howard! I want to go home."

There was the far-off buzz of a chain saw and the rustling of the leaves on the nearby trees, but no human sound at all apart from her own breathing.

Ruth picked up her bag and positioned it on her back to begin the long walk into town. She didn't blame Howard for leaving, but the trip home wasn't going to be much fun.

She hadn't gotten far when she heard a shout behind her.

"Hey, Craze!"

Ruth turned around in surprise but couldn't see anyone. Who else but Howard called her *Craze*? She walked back toward the river and, sure enough, there was Howard running across the bridge toward her.

So he hadn't ditched her! They'd be able to go home together.

"Wait!" he shouted. "You're not going to believe this!" He was holding something quite big high up in the air, yelling excitedly as he ran toward her. "Wait!"

"I *am* waiting, Pope, you idiot!"

"You are not going to believe this!"

"You caught a fish?"

"Better!"

Ruth had never seen Howard run before, or sound so animated. He was across the bridge now and still running. Ruth finally saw what he was holding.

No. This was too weird.

"I found him, Craze!" Howard rushed up to her. "See, I found him!"

He thrust a battered, dusty Rodney into her hands and then collapsed on the ground to catch his breath.

Ruth stared down at the rat, trying to mesh this battered toy with the Rodney she knew. Well, he'd told her, hadn't he? He'd said he'd bow out if she chose to come back the third time. She wanted to cry suddenly.

One of his eyes was missing and the other was hanging by a thread. His jacket was half rotted away and he'd lost a boot. His whole right side was covered in thick dry mud. Ruth couldn't speak.

"It is him, isn't it?" Howard asked, scrambling to his feet. "That's your rat, right?"

"Yeah, it's him."

"I found him in a dry eddy upstream from the bridge," Howard explained. "I thought it was an old shirt or something and I didn't take any notice of it until I was about to go home. Then, when I picked it up, well . . . I ran all the way back."

"Thanks." Ruth was still too confused to respond properly.

"The poor little guy," Howard mumbled, scratching off a

bit of mud from Rodney's boot. "No one's taken care of him for a while." He looked up at her. "I told you we'd find him, didn't I?"

"You did, Howard." Ruth smiled at her pale, odd-looking friend and hugged his thin shoulders quickly and fiercely. "Thanks."

Howard shrugged her off, but his face had colored with pleasure.

"You going to take him home?" he asked gruffly.

"Of course I am." Ruth undid the strap of her bag and gently put Rodney inside.

The four-kilometer walk back from the bridge into town seemed much longer than the trip out. Only one car passed, without even slowing down. A number of times Ruth was on the verge of telling Howard about all that had happened to her that day, but it seemed too big somehow, a little too crazy.

By the time they reached the bus stop, Ruth's feet were aching so much, she thought there was a chance they might fall off. She and Howard were thirsty as well as hungry. Not to mention cold. They tried to joke as they waited for the bus, hopping up and down to keep their toes warm, but it was a long, chilly wait, and the jokes petered out.

Eventually, the bus came. Ruth and Howard slumped into a double seat halfway down. Howard took the window seat again, but Ruth didn't mind much. She had a pretty good view from her seat.

"I found the rat too," she said quietly, once the bus was on its way.

"How do you mean?" Howard turned to her, puzzled.

"This afternoon, I found Rodney."

Howard stared at her. "What?"

"It's a long story."

"Do I look like I'm busy?" Howard gave one of his sudden grins, which made Ruth smile back immediately. She really liked the way his face could change so quickly. He was a weird little old man–boy until he smiled. Then he turned into a normal kid.

Ruth ended up giving Howard a detailed account of what had happened to her that day. He kept very quiet most of the time. Occasionally, he grunted or sighed or looked agitated in a way that made her think he might be finding it all a bit too much.

"Howard, I'm not making this up," Ruth felt compelled to say a couple of times.

"Didn't say you were," he said sharply. "So, this happened when I was *asleep*?"

"Partly. Then when you went fishing."

Howard didn't reply; he just looked at her.

"I'm *not* a nutcase," she said. "I wouldn't believe it either, except it happened to me."

"Not saying you are a nutcase," Howard mumbled.

"So what do you think?"

But he only shrugged.

She tried not to care.

They both sat back and stared out the window.

After a while Ruth relaxed a bit. She liked the feeling of skimming along the black road, with the rush of lights as the stops were announced. It was a clear evening, the moon was up already, and they were cocooned in a warm tin can that was hurtling along in space.

Ruth's spirits soared with it. Telling Howard everything had loosened the anxious knot that had been with her most of the day, and, quite inexplicably, she was *excited* to be going home.

23

When they rounded the corner across from her house, Ruth noticed that the porch light was on. Did that mean the family was home or . . . not? The place really didn't look so bad. Sure, the roof sagged and her father had left a large piece of machinery on the veranda, and even from this distance she could see the shabbiness of the peeling weatherboards, but— maybe just because it was nighttime and the darkness softened the impact—the whole place looked sort of . . . *friendly*.

Together, Ruth and Howard walked up to the front door. Ruth took out her key and tried to act normal, but her heart was beating fast and her mouth was dry. She was so glad to be home, but what would she say? What *could* she say? The truth would sound way too crazy and yet . . . how could she not tell the truth? She walked down the hallway, Howard behind her, took a deep breath, and pushed open the kitchen door.

"Hey, everyone! I'm back," she yelled.

But there was no one there. The kitchen was empty and cold, just as she'd left it that morning. Ruth didn't know whether to be pleased or not. It meant that at least for now she didn't have to explain herself, but ... she'd been looking forward to seeing them.

"So where are they?" Howard asked.

"Not back yet."

"Any food?"

"I'll have a look."

But there wasn't much to eat, no bread left in the tin and no pies in the freezer, and they'd taken all the cheese and the fruit with them that day. There was nothing for it but to heat up an old can of celery soup and eat it with some dry biscuits.

They were both still hungry at the end of their meal. Ruth could tell by the way that Howard was shifting around in his seat that he was also still sore from the beating his father had given him, so she suggested a bath with some of her mother's soothing bath oils. To her surprise, he agreed and seemed quite intrigued by the idea. Ruth ran the bath, and then left him to it. She went out the back door and stood looking at the backyard. The sky was clear now, and cold. She sat down on the back step and patted the dog.

Howard was still in the bath when Ruth heard the car pull up outside. There was a loud horn blast and then a succession of slamming doors, wild whoops and shouts. The front door burst open and her brothers ran in, followed by her parents.

"Hello, Ruthie!" Mrs. Craze called cheerfully. "You hungry, love?"

"Yes!" The delicious aroma of fish and chips hit Ruth's nostrils. When she spied the two steaming packages in her mother's tote bag, her mouth began to water. She hugged her mother and then her father, who was holding bottles of milk and soft drink. Marcus was taking off his shoes and dumping his coat on the floor, but when he saw Ruth he stopped.

"You should have been there today, sis!" he boasted. "You missed the race of a lifetime!"

"Did you get into the finals?"

"Do one-legged ducks swim in circles?"

"Hey," Ruth said with a smile, "congratulations." For the first time in ages she really meant it.

"Can we eat now, Mum?" Paul whined. "Before we have to put stuff away?"

"Good idea." Mrs. Craze laughed, ruffling his hair. "Let's do that."

"I could eat a horse and chase the jockey!" Marcus shouted.

Suddenly, the unmistakable sound of running water came from the bathroom. They all turned to look at Ruth.

"Who's in there?"

"My friend Howard Pope," Ruth said. "He's got sore legs."

"Is he that new boy from school?" Mrs. Craze asked with a frown.

Ruth nodded. "His father beat him really badly, so I told him he could have a bath," she said.

"Oh, that's a good idea, Ruthie," her mother said, looking worriedly at her husband.

"I pinched your special healing oils," Ruth confessed.

"That's fine, love." Her mother sighed. All the excitement had drained from her face. "I've heard things about that boy's father," she said quietly, "up at the school. Ken, we've got to do something. Help him in some way."

"I'm not sure if we can, dear," Mr. Craze said warily.

"We must," Mrs. Craze said. "Don't you think, Ruthie?"

Ruth nodded. "Yeah," she said gruffly.

Somewhat subdued now, the family moved down the hallway into the warmth of the kitchen, and Ruth slipped upstairs to check on Howard.

"Hurry up, Howard," she shouted through the bathroom door. "Everyone's home and there's fish and chips!"

By the time the family was seated at the table, the glasses filled with drink, the packages unwrapped, Howard had appeared in the doorway.

"Come in, Howard!" Mr. Craze pulled out a seat between

himself and Paul and handed him a glass of soft drink. "It's a free-for-all here, so I suggest you don't hold back!"

"Welcome, Howard!" Mrs. Craze smiled. "Please eat. There's loads here."

"Thanks," Howard muttered, looking at the fish and chips hungrily but not moving.

Mrs. Craze grabbed the tongs and served him a generous amount. "You see how you go with that," she said kindly, handing him the bottle of tomato sauce.

Howard bent his head and began to wolf down the food.

Mrs. Craze was right. There was easily enough to feed six hungry people on a cold night.

Too busy eating, no one spoke for some time. Ruth finished first, and she looked around the table from one person to the next, noticing how content and happy everyone seemed as they ate.

When the fish and chips were finished, Mrs. Craze screwed up the paper and threw it in the bin.

"No dishes tonight, Ruthie!" She beamed.

Ruth thought of the perfect version of her mother—the one with the dead eyes—and shuddered involuntarily. *Imagine if she'd stayed there!*

Mrs. Craze was at the fridge. "Now, who's for ice cream?"

"Yes, please!" Everyone wanted ice cream.

"So, what sort of day did you have, Ruthie?" her father asked casually. "How is Lou's grandfather?"

There was a lull in the noise and bustle around the table. Everyone stopped talking to hear. Ruth had almost forgotten her lie of that morning and certainly hadn't decided what she was going to say. She swallowed a mouthful of ice cream and looked at Howard. He was studying the spoon in his hand. She looked at both her parents and sighed.

"I lied about that," she said. "He isn't sick at all."

"What?" Marcus stared at her.

"Close your mouth while you're eating, Marcus," Ruth snapped, then turned to her parents. "I didn't go to see Lou while her parents were at the hospital."

"Huh, I told you they hated each other!" Marcus said. "So that makes Ruth a . . . liar!"

"Be quiet, Marcus," Mr. Craze said sternly. "What do you mean, Ruth?"

"I lied," she said again. "I went to look for Rodney."

"For *who*?"

"For Rodney . . . the rat."

"You went *where*?" Mrs. Craze was openmouthed.

"To the creek," Ruth said, feeling her face getting hotter. She looked at Marcus. "To where we last saw him."

"But that was . . . months ago! And such a long way!"

Ruth said nothing, but she wasn't hungry anymore. She gave

the rest of her ice cream to Paul, who was delighted. "Thanks, Ruthie."

"How did you get there?"

"Bus and train."

"Well." Mrs. Craze frowned and put down her spoon.

"Well." Mr. Craze nodded thoughtfully, as though trying to process the information. "That is pretty . . . surprising, Ruth, I have to say." He looked blankly at his wife. "So did you *find* him?" he said at last.

"Yes."

"Well, I suppose that's something, but . . ." Mr. Craze seemed baffled more than anything.

"But you shouldn't have lied about it, Ruth," Mrs. Craze said. "That really wasn't good of you. You could have . . . I mean, what if we . . . What if something had happened?"

"I know . . . I'm sorry."

"It was my idea," Howard cut in. They all turned to look at him.

"Well, it was Ruth's decision, Howard," Mrs. Craze said kindly, "so I don't think you are responsible." Everyone was quiet as she stood up, collected the glasses, and dumped them in the sink. "Did you go too, Howard?"

"Yes." Howard nodded. "It was the best day of my life."

"Oh." Mrs. Craze smiled helplessly, moved because he was so obviously sincere. Instead of sitting down again, she stood behind Ruth and drew her hair back from her face the way she used to when Ruth was a little girl. "What will we do with you, Ruthie?" she said softly.

Ruth shrugged, closed her eyes, and sighed.

"Put her in a dark room," Marcus said quickly, "with only bread and water!"

"Make her lie on a bed of nails!" Paul shouted.

In the end they were all laughing.

"Can Howard stay?" Paul wanted to know an hour later. "*Please*, Mum."

They'd been playing a board game until Mrs. Craze announced it was time for bed. "I *need* him here in the morning so we can finish the game."

"Would you like to stay, Howard?" Mrs. Craze asked. "Or would you like us to drive you home?"

"I'd like to stay," he said shyly, "if it's okay."

"Of course it is, but . . . I take it your father knows where you are?"

There was a moment's awkward silence. Howard shook his head. "Not really."

Howard didn't want to ring home, and in the end Mr. Craze offered to do it. The phone call didn't last long, and Mr. Craze had a slightly stunned expression on his face when he held out the phone to Howard.

"Your dad would like a word," he said quietly.

They all waited to see what the verdict would be. They could hear a loud voice on the other end but nothing much of what was actually being said. Howard just stood there passively, saying *yes* and *no* a few times and then a quick mumbled *good-bye*. He put the phone down and turned to Ruth's parents.

"It's okay," he said, his face blank. "I can stay."

Without a word, Mrs. Craze made him up a bed on the big couch in the family room.

24

Back in her room, Ruth took Rodney out of her bag and put him up on his old shelf. Once in bed herself, she looked at him and smiled.

"It's good to have you back," she whispered. But there was no answer. Not even a flicker of an eyelid.

There was a small knock at her door, and her mother's head appeared.

"Night, Ruthie," she said.

"Night, Mum. And thanks for . . . everything."

"*Everything?*" Her mother grinned.

"Well, for being kind to Howard and . . ." Ruth sighed. "The rest of it."

"That's okay." Mrs. Craze was about to disappear when Ruth thought of something that had been in the back of her mind all day.

"Mum, can you remember the lady who gave Mary Ellen the rat?"

"Oh yes." Mrs. Craze came back into the room. "It was Mrs. Bee next door."

"But what was her real name?"

Her mother frowned and thought for a moment. Then her eyes brightened.

"Bridie," she said. "She was a lovely lady. Very close to Mary Ellen. Why did you want to know, love?"

"Did Bridie have things from China too?"

Mrs. Craze turned away, looking thoughtful for a few moments. "Yes, now that you mention it," she said. "She had lovely vases and little ornaments. Children's toys. It was Bridie who first got Mary Ellen interested in China. Bridie had these lovely exotic things around her house that fascinated Mary Ellen but … how on earth did you know?"

Ruth could hardly speak, her head was in such a whirl. "Can I tell you another time, Mum?" she managed. "I'm so tired now."

Mrs. Craze walked over to the bed and gave Ruth a quick, hard hug.

"Good night, my one and only wicked girl."

Ruth laughed.

"Good night, my one and only crazy mother."

Maybe two hours later, Ruth woke up with a start, her heart hammering. Something didn't feel right. She'd forgotten to pull down her blind, and moonlight had flooded the room.

Had something happened? Had she been dreaming? Her first impulse was to check on Rodney. Yes, there he was. She could see him sitting up there on the top shelf in exactly the same position. She didn't even have to switch on the light because of the moon. So why did she feel so churned up and . . . uneasy? She pushed back the blankets and put both feet on the cold floor.

She knew what she had to do.

She slipped on her jeans, shirt, and sweater, picked up Rodney from the shelf, and put him back in her bag. Carrying her coat and shoes in one hand and the bag in the other she tiptoed out into the family room.

Howard was lying flat on his back on the couch, arms by his sides and dead to the world.

"Hey," she whispered, touching his shoulder. "Wake up."

He opened his eyes, blinked a couple of times, and looked at her quietly. He was so *unsurprised* that Ruth laughed under her breath. It was almost like he'd been waiting for her.

"Get dressed," she said. "We've got to do something."

They walked through the quiet backstreets down to the river that Ruth and Mary Ellen used to walk along on their way home from the city. Scooting down the embankment, they found the right path and from there it was only a short distance to the bridge over the train tracks. Ruth knew Howard must be tired.

She was pretty tired herself. But he never complained, nor even asked what they were doing.

At last they arrived. They stood in the middle of the footbridge and looked down onto the tracks. Ruth thought of the last time she'd come to this spot with her aunt. She could see her in her red coat and black boots, her hair tucked under a felt hat and her face so pale. She'd had her first operation and was having chemotherapy. Ruth hadn't had any idea how serious it was then, but Mary Ellen must have known.

"Will you come here sometimes?" Mary Ellen had taken her arm. "When you're big?"

"Of course."

"And think of me?"

"Yes." Ruth had looked at her aunt. It wasn't like her to get all mushy.

"I'll be here whenever you come back," her aunt had persisted.

"But what if you're doing something else?"

"I'll be here in spirit."

"Okay."

Mary Ellen had kissed the top of her head. And it was at that point that they'd heard the faint rumble on the tracks. They grinned and closed their eyes. Louder and louder it roared toward them, and then it thundered past and was gone.

They'd looked at each other expectantly.

"You first," Ruth said quickly.

Mary Ellen laughed and put an arm around her shoulders. "Wings," Mary Ellen said matter-of-factly. "Wings that I can fit onto my feet."

"Wings for your *feet*?" Ruth loved the idea immediately. She could imagine them sprouting out the back of her aunt's dainty feet, just above the heel. "Would you be able to fly with them?"

"Oh, definitely." Mary Ellen laughed again. "And still have my hands free. I could carry things up into the clouds. I could piggyback you, for example."

"Cool!"

"Come on, kiddo, or we'll be late for your tea."

They had turned around then and started on the walk home.

Howard watched as Ruth undid her bag and pulled out the battered rat and held him up to face the moon.

"Good-bye, Rodney," she told the rat sternly.

"What are you doing?" Howard was alarmed. "We just found him!"

"And he's yours now."

"What?"

"Yours."

Ruth thrust Rodney into Howard's arms.

"But . . ."

"Until he stops being useful, and then . . . you pass him on. Is that clear?"

Howard smiled. It was a beautiful smile, unlike any that Ruth had seen him give before.

"You for real, Craze?"

Ruth nodded. She could hear a rumble on the tracks. It must be the 11:53—the last train of the night. The next would be the 5:03 in the morning. "Howard, quick! Close your eyes and make a wish."

Ruth closed her own eyes as the train rattled past, and although she couldn't see anything, she had a very strong feeling that her aunt was on it, standing at the carriage window, looking out and smiling. Mary Ellen was glad Ruth was who she was, and no one else.

Ruth let the relief roll through her. This place had worked its magic just as she knew it would. It wasn't as if she had all her friends back or her aunt was alive again. It wasn't as though she had a perfect house or family, or that she was famous or more special than her brothers. But somehow, she did feel lucky again. And that was something. It really was.

"Okay?" Howard asked.

"I think so," Ruth replied. "Did you make a wish?"

Maureen McCarthy

is a bestselling author in her native Australia. Her books include *Cross My Heart* (short-listed for four literary awards), *Chain of Hearts* (short-listed for the Ethel Turner Prize for Young People's Literature), *Rose by Any Other Name*, and *Somebody's Crying*.

This book was designed by Robyn Ng and art directed by Chad W. Beckerman. The text is set in 10-point The Serif Light, Light Plain, a typeface first published by Luc de Groot in 1994 as part of a larger family of fonts called Thesis. The display type is Memimas.

This book was printed and bound by R. R. Donnelley in Crawfordsville, Indiana. Its production was overseen by Alison Gervais.